The Crossing

♡ Taylor Joseph

Published by:
Four Star Publishing
P.O. Box 871784
Canton, MI 48187
fourstarpublishing@comcast.net

ISBN: 978-0-9815894-0-4

Cover and interior design and layout by Lee Lewis Walsh, Words Plus Design, www.wordsplusdesign.com

Printed in the United States of America

The Crossing

a novel by

TAYLOR JOSEPH
WITH LAWRENCE JOSEPH

FOUR STAR PUBLISHING
CANTON, MICHIGAN

— 1 —

The door slammed from our rundown, one bedroom house. The noise startled me as I looked up. There was my mother again, just like she had been a hundred times before, surveying the yard to see if everything was normal. She walked over to the clothesline, which held the few garments that we owned. She signaled me to come to her. As I slowly rose and approached her, she said, "Help me with the clothes because I have to go into town in a little while."

Her faded dress was slightly torn near the bottom and was a pale blue from the many days it had been worn. Her hands were dry and chapped from a lifetime of hard work and neglect. She turned to me and said, "Maria, I hope it goes well in town today."

Mama had gone to town many times before. Sometimes she would come home with nothing but a sad look on her face. And sometimes she would come home with enough food to feed us for days. My mother always seemed to find a way to get food or whatever we needed.

The fact is, we lived in an area where there weren't many jobs and most people just struggled to survive. We often thought of moving closer to Mexico City so Mama could get a good paying job, but we just didn't have enough money to move there.

If we moved, we would have to leave our home on foot, carrying what little we owned, hoping she would find a job right away. If she didn't, we would be living on the streets. My mother always said, "It's probably better to stay where we are, because at least we have a roof over our heads."

We lived in a rural area seventy miles west of Monterrey, Mexico. Monterrey is located approximately 300 miles south of the border of the United States, directly below Texas. The area in which we live is considered a self-supporting poor area in northern Mexico. Most of the people do not have much. They just get by any way they can.

My mother is five feet, four inches tall with long, dark brown hair. She has beautiful, big brown eyes which are always a welcome sight to me. She has a nice thin body and weighs about 110 pounds. Her name is Anita Perez. I always thought this was a fitting name for her, one that complemented her immensely.

I always thought she was pretty, despite her worn, tattered clothes and her dry, chapped hands. Mama had never had a new dress, since I could remember, and neither did I. I knew she was trying hard to provide for us, so the feeling I had of doing without seemed all right. Sometimes when things wouldn't go well for us, she would say, "We need to be thankful, because this is our life and that's the way things are."

She was always kind to me and I knew she loved me. Before she left for town, I thought about asking her again. I had reluctantly asked her many times before. The answer was always no. She never backed down and she never gave in. I wondered if I had enough courage to ask her today. I wanted to wait until the timing was just right.

We folded our last shirt, then Mama said, "Come on, Maria. It is time to come in. I have to go into town now." My heart raced in anticipation of her answer. Was this the day she would finally say yes? As I walked in, I looked up at the water-stained ceiling of our house, which showed many years of leakage and wear. I wondered just how many years it would be before we would be able to get a new roof. It did not rain often where we lived, so our roof didn't really leak much. When it did rain, though, we would get occasional drips through the roof.

In our living room we had an old, comfortable, gray sofa that I felt like I had grown up with. Near the sofa was a small chair and an old wooden end table by its side. The living room was connected to the kitchen, and in the kitchen was a small wooden table where we ate all our meals.

We didn't have any modern appliances, just a wood-burning stove that we rarely used to cook. We had a small refrigerator that barely kept our food cold, which we had owned since I could remember. The walls were made of thin wood that showed the wear from the stifling heat and sun of our long Mexican summers.

My mother's bedroom had a single bed with a dresser next to it. It had a small chair up against the wall, where she loved to read when she could. The bedroom had one small window over the bed, which let in a small amount of light.

The entire house had a dull, faded, wooden floor that creaked when you walked across it. In the middle of the small living room, there was an old brown rug with tattered fringe on the ends. The rug had been there since I could remember. There were two small windows in the living room that were old but usable. Mama was so proud that after all these years, ours was one of the only houses in the neighborhood with windows that had never been broken.

Our yard was small with long, grassy weeds that my mother used to cut by hand with a sickle. In the summer, though, she never had to cut the grass much because the temperature would rise to over 100 degrees. This made the grass die.

Our entire house was no larger than twenty feet long by twenty-five feet wide. There were twenty houses similar to ours in a row on our street. The people in our neighborhood were no better off than us, or no worse.

The thought ran across my mind again about how I would ask Mama that important question. She was in her bedroom, dressing, while I thought of what I would say. I peered in her room nervously and said, "Mama, I was wondering if I could go into town with you today."

She turned to me and said, "Maria Perez. You know the market is no place for a twelve-year-old girl to be all day long."

I had medium brown hair and a thin body. I was of average height, about four feet, nine inches tall. I had two crooked teeth on the left side of my mouth, which were not really noticeable unless I smiled. I had deep brown eyes, like almost everyone I knew.

I said, "That's right, I'm twelve years old and I'm ready to go with you."

She said, "Absolutely not. I have to see if some of the vendors will allow me to help at their booths today. I don't think it will go over well if I have a child with me. And besides, I'm not leaving you alone at the marketplace."

I started to say, "I know, but—"

She put her finger to her lips and said, "Shush, not another word. You can't go into town with me and that's final."

I couldn't help but feel that if I could go to the marketplace with her, I could help her earn some money. If she would just give me a chance, I would show her how helpful I could be.

When she was finally ready to leave, she said, "Remember, you have many chores to do around here. I can't do everything and find work at the same time. Don't forget to get water from the well so we can wash clothes tomorrow. And don't forget to go to Gaupy's farm and see if they need any help."

Sometimes during the summer I would work at Gaupy's farm and earn some extra money to help Mama. We needed all the money we could get and, besides, I didn't really mind. The problem was that many other children from the area would go to the local farms and try to earn money also, which made it hard sometimes. I was only able to get work there once in a while, but I still had to try. I made the three mile walk to the farm almost daily in the summer in hopes of earning some money just to help out.

Just then Mama said, "Are you listening to me? I have a five mile walk to town and I should be home by 7:00 p.m. Please behave. I love you."

It never sat well with me that my mother wouldn't take me to the marketplace with her. I really wanted to go with her, but for now I would just have to wait until I was older.

I reluctantly walked out to the yard to get the buckets so I could get water from the well. The well was located at the end of our small, dusty yard, right by the one-lane dirt road in front of our house.

In the summer, I would bring the full buckets of water in the house and empty them into a large plastic storage container. It was crucial that we kept this container full, so we could do our laundry and dishes. The container held nearly forty buckets of water, which I would have to fill almost daily. I really didn't mind filling the container because it was something that had to be done. I knew Mama worked hard, so I would do whatever I could to help out.

The full heat of the day had not set in yet. I knew that the sooner I got that barrel filled up with water, the better. Soon the stifling heat would hinder my ability to work. I knew it would take much longer to fill, the later it got. As I proceeded through the yard with my first set of buckets, José, a friend of mine, asked me if I wanted to play soccer with him.

José was an eleven-year-old boy with jet black hair. He had a friendly, nice smile, and was wearing a faded pair of blue jean shorts and the same red shirt he usually wore.

José was a little smaller than most children his age, but it didn't seem to bother him much. The fact that José had a soccer ball was impressive. No one in our neighborhood could afford much of anything, let alone a soccer ball. Out of all the children that lived in our neighborhood, he was the only kid that had one.

When José asked a friend if he or she wanted to kick the ball with him, the friend almost always lit up with the biggest smile and blurted out "yes" before he could finish asking. I told José, "I can't right now, because I have to get water from the well."

He said "Are you sure you can't play with me, just for a minute?"

I said, "Well, only for a minute, because I have so much to do and I can't afford to get behind."

I loved playing soccer and just couldn't resist. The ball was white with brown spots and a rough, worn cover that showed many hours of use. José had gotten the ball as a gift from his uncle two years ago at Christmas. It was slightly under-inflated, which made the ball float a little when you kicked it.

José and I spent a few minutes passing the ball back and forth. Then I told him I had to leave. He tried to convince me to play longer, but I told him I couldn't. I picked up my buckets, hurried to the well, and started pumping. It took about twenty minutes to fill the entire barrel to the top. When I was done, I was tired and hot, so I sat down for a short rest.

Before I knew it, I fell asleep and woke to the sound of the neighbor's door slamming. I rushed up as if someone had lit a firecracker underneath me. I knew I should have already been on my way to the farm to see if I could get work.

By this time, the temperature had reached the mid-90s and I knew that the walk would not be a pleasant one in the enveloping heat. As I walked, I dreamed about living in California. I dreamed about being able to buy Mama anything she wanted. I remembered all the days that I had gone to bed hungry without an evening meal. Just then, a thought popped into my head about the stories I'd heard about people that lived in mansions in the United States. They were able to eat whatever they wanted as often as they liked.

As I approached the halfway point to the farm, I could feel my short brown hair blowing in the wind. A bead of sweat from my forehead ran into my eyes. That made them sting a little, but since I had made that walk many times before, my body was used to the stifling heat and the long walk.

As I approached the farm, I saw that someone was walking on the road toward me. As the person came closer, I recognized Vanessa. She was an eleven-year-old girl that lived a few houses away from me.

The tan dress that she wore frequently had a small tear in it just above her knees and looked dirty and old. I knew she was probably happy just to have it, though. As she approached me, I asked her if there was work at the farm. She said, "No."

I asked her if she would walk back to the farm with me, and she said, "No."

I was going to go to the farm anyway, just in case. I continued down the road in the scorching heat, thinking that the temperature had to be approaching 100 degrees.

Upon arriving at the farm, I saw two children that had been lucky enough to get work that day. I went and found the farm leader and asked him, "Is there any work that needs to be done today?" He replied, "I'm sorry, Maria, but we only had enough work for two children today. We gave it to the children that came here earlier."

A sad feeling came over me and my stomach felt a little tight. I knew, deep inside, that I might have been the one who got the work, if I hadn't fallen asleep, and if I hadn't played ball with José. I told him, "Thank you. I'll be back tomorrow."

As I turned to walk back home, the farm leader called out, "Be here earlier tomorrow, because we're going to need four children." I thanked him and started to leave.

The farm leader's name was Jesse. He had always been fair to me in the past. He always tried to make sure I could work at the farm whenever possible. He was a large man about six feet tall, with brown hair, a beard, a mustache, and kind, dark eyes. He had a tan cowboy hat on and black boots that had a slight point at the ends.

I felt the reason he was kind to me was because he knew my mother well, and he had known my father, Miguel, before he died. Jesse had gone to school with my father when they were young. The fact that my father had died and left Mama and me alone might have been why he favored me when there was work to be given out.

My mother had told me that Jesse had been at my father's funeral and had been very helpful after he died. The fact that I was late today was probably the main reason why there was no work at the farm for me.

I never really knew my father, because he died when I was two years old. Mama always told me, "He was a good man with a kind heart. " She always said that she missed him very much. I couldn't help but think of how our lives would be so much different if he was still alive. She had a few pictures of him when he was a boy, and only two of them when they were married.

I loved hearing stories about when she was little and how things were when she was growing up. Sometimes when I asked her to tell me stories about my father, she would, but sometimes she would say, "Not today." I think at times it was too painful for her to relive the past.

My father had been a short man, only five feet, seven inches tall. He had brown hair, brown eyes, and a small mole on his left cheek. At least, this is how he looked from the few pictures I had seen of him. I know my mother had been in love with him, and I know it was very hard on her when he died. The fact that he died so suddenly, in a car accident, must have been extremely hard for her to handle.

Mama was only twenty-three years old when my father died, and she was left with me to support by herself. It must have been absolutely terrifying for her to be left alone at such a young age. She must have been grief-stricken for months after his death. To this day, she would rarely talk about the months following his death.

My mother really did love me and I loved her, too. I knew it was she and I against the world, and I was determined to do whatever I could to help.

My train of thought was quickly broken as a truck came speeding down the road to the farm with supplies. I realized that I had better get back home soon. Since there was no work on the farm for me that day, there was no point of me hanging around.

On the way out, I took a long drink from the well. The temperature had risen to over 100 degrees by now. It was noon, and I knew the hottest part of the day was still to come, between 3:00 and 4:00 p.m.

I reluctantly began to walk toward home as the sun beat down on me. Normally, this walk was one of the hardest parts of the day. After working at the farm for four or more hours in the excessive heat, the three mile walk was absolutely exhausting. Today it wouldn't be quite as bad because I hadn't worked.

As I proceeded down the long dusty road, thoughts of being rich and living in a mansion rushed through my head again. I hoped Mama would be home when I got there, although usually she wasn't.

I wondered how she would do at the market today. I wondered if she would bring food home or if we would be eating something we had from the previous day. I remembered how once, she had worked two full days at the booths and she brought home some hamburger, a few potatoes, two large bottles of fresh milk, two loaves of bread, and a bag of carrots. We ate well for two days. I will never forget how I felt when I sat down and ate that first meal.

I believed that things should have been like that every day for us. We could have eaten like that all the time if my father hadn't died. He used to be a general laborer at a farm that was twenty miles away and usually worked steady. Mama had told me that since he died, it had been a constant struggle.

Just then I heard a noise in the distance. I turned to look and saw that it was the supply truck returning from the farm. The truck looked like a huge dust ball rolling down the road. As the driver approached, I noticed him slowing down.

The large truck was approximately twenty years old with brown rust spots all over the doors and fenders. It was light green in color, which you could hardly see because of the dirt that accumulated on the sides. The truck bed had many boxes filled with farming tools and supplies.

The driver stopped, rolled down his window, and said, "It's too hot for anybody to be walking today. Would you like a ride?" I immediately said "yes."

The driver's name was Javier. He had known my mother for fifteen years, so I was familiar with him. He had been over to our house on several occasions, so I didn't hesitate to say "yes." He was about six feet tall, with shoulder length dark hair. He had a thick, bushy mustache that made him look a little funny. He wore a plaid shirt, blue jeans, a straw cowboy hat and cowboy boots. As I got into the truck, I noticed a heavy smell of tobacco that lingered in the air. Javier was a pretty nice man and had given me a ride many times before. One time he took me all the way to my house.

I was just happy I didn't have to walk down that road in the sweltering heat. As I got in the truck, I remembered how I used to bounce up and down on the seat because the road was so bumpy. This time was no different.

As we approached the end of the road where my street intersected, Javier asked me, "Is your mother home?"

As I opened the door of the dust-covered truck I said, "No, but thank you for the ride." By this time it was nearly 4:00 p.m. and I was hungry.

Mama had left me some crackers and a small apple for lunch. I couldn't wait to get in so I could eat the small but welcome portion of food. I knew she wouldn't be home until 5:30 or possibly even later. I carefully took out the crackers and the apple and slowly began to eat. I remembered just how delicious five crackers and an apple could taste after I took the first bite.

After I was done eating, I went outside and got a huge glass of water from the well. As I gulped it down, Rafael, a seven-year-old boy from the neighborhood, was passing by.

He was one of the smallest seven-year-olds I had ever seen. He had light brown hair, with hazel eyes and tiny feet. He said, "Come on, Maria, let's go! José wants to play soccer down at the field."

When José went down to the field with his soccer ball, all the children would come out and play. It wasn't often that we would get the chance to have that much fun. So I said, "I'll be right there." The fact that the temperature was over 100 degrees didn't matter much, because we loved soccer and we would usually take long breaks.

I rushed into my house and wrote Mama a note saying, "I'm down at the field playing soccer," and rushed out. As I hurried down to the end of the field, I wondered if I was going to get a chance to play right away, or if I would have to wait. Upon arriving at the field, I realized that I would have a good chance to play right away because there were only eleven children there. This made uneven teams.

The field was dirty with scraggly grass that had burned up from the penetrating heat. The field itself was small with two garbage cans at each end for goals. The kids were just picking teams when I arrived. I was picked to be on José's team, which pleased me immensely. We played soccer off and on in the heat for about an hour.

Most of the children I knew were no better off than me. Most of the parents struggled to provide food and clothing for their families. Most of my friends that played soccer that day owned only one pair of shoes.

By now, it was nearly 6:00 p.m. and the temperature was still near 100 degrees. After playing soccer, I was drenched with sweat. I went over to the well to wash my face and hands. The water felt great as I splashed it upon my head and took a long drink to replenish my body. I knew my mother would be home any time now. I hoped she'd had a good day at the market and would bring home a decent meal.

I walked back to my house and sat out in the front yard waiting for Mama to arrive. The light summer breeze blew through my hair, cooling me off somewhat. I waited about fifteen minutes and I saw a figure in the distance. As the figure approached, I realized it was my mother.

At that moment, I sprinted toward her. I yelled, "Mama, Mama, I'm happy to see you. Did you bring home any food with you?"

She gave me a big hug and said, "Some." She had a brown paper bag in her hands, which I knew had to have something good in it.

My heart raced with excitement about what she had in the bag. I remembered all the times she had come home and brought full meals with her. I remembered how happy we were when we sat down to eat dinner. But then a thought popped into my head about all the times when she didn't bring home a full meal. These were times when we had to do without.

As I shuffled into the house, I felt a thick, uncomfortable lump in my throat from anxiety. Mama told me to get some plates and cups out of the cupboard. As I did, she set some silverware on the table. She turned to me with a reproving look on her face and said, "Maria, we have to be thankful for what we have."

I knew from the tone of her voice and the look on her face that she probably didn't have a huge meal. She said, "I tried to get work all afternoon at the vendors. It was very slow, but I did the best I could. How did you do today? Was there any work at the farm?"

I replied, "No." I didn't have the heart to tell her that I had been late to the farm because I fell asleep, but I knew there had been only enough work for two children that day. So I would not have been working anyway.

Mama reached into the bag and pulled out half a loaf of bread, two apples, a banana, three small pieces of salami, six crackers, and a small cup of milk. We said our blessings, split the food, and began to eat. My mother put half of the bread, one apple, one piece of salami, and the crackers away for tomorrow. We split the banana, the bread, and the salami between us. Mama gave me the entire cup of milk.

As I gobbled my food down, she snapped at me, "Maria, I have told you a thousand times to eat slowly and not gobble your food down." I told her that I would try to eat slower. I was really hungry and knew it would be difficult, though.

A pleasant thought popped into my head as I was finishing up my meal. I remembered that Antonio, a friend of Mama's, would come over from time to time and drop off small amounts of food for us. He came over whenever he could, usually about once a week. Antonio had been a good friend of my father's before he died.

When he would bring us food, he told us we should accept anything that he gave us. He would say, "I enjoy bringing you food. I was such good friends with your father, it is the least I can do to help." He also said that giving was the Lord's work. I hoped today would be one of those days.

After we were done with our meal, I was still hungry. Usually when I would eat, I would feel full half an hour after I was done eating. I knew today would be different, though. As I cleared the table, I thought that at least doing the dishes would be easy today. The fact that there wasn't much food made it an easy night to clean up. I only had two small brown plastic cups, two old plastic yellow plates, and the silverware to clean.

After the dishes were done, I asked Mama, "Tell me more about my father."

She said, "Maria, I've told you a million times about your father. Maybe we will talk about him right before we go to bed."

I'm sure Mama knew that I had seen her many times crying at night after I went to bed. One time I had asked her why she was crying and she said, "I miss your father and I wish he were still here."

Before bed, we always prayed and thanked God for everything we had. I think sometimes she cried because we didn't have enough food or other things that we needed. But Mama always claimed this was not the case and she was crying because she felt alone without my father. A day didn't go by when we didn't wonder how much better life would be if he was still alive.

On many occasions, Mama told me he had been a great man. She said, "He was a very hard-working, kind, understanding, and loving man." Even though she didn't want to tell me a story at that moment, I knew I could persuade her to tell me one later.

Usually after dinner, Mama and I would go for a walk. Sometimes I enjoyed going to see what the other kids were doing at night in the neighborhood. One strict rule was that I could play only if all the work was done.

As we began to move toward the door, Mama asked, "Do you want to go for a long walk or a short one?" I almost always said a long one. Our neighborhood was safe, even though numerous poor families lived there. Everyone knew each other and helped one another if they could.

By now, most of the families would be finished with dinner. I thought we might see one or two of my friends during our walk. I hoped I would see José. I had always thought he was special. He was one of the only friends I had that I just loved to be around, even though there really wasn't much time for fun, except for an occasional soccer game.

As we walked out the door, it was about 9:00. The sun was just about to set and the temperature had cooled down to the upper 80s. Our walk would sometimes last for up to an hour, depending on how much we talked. Tonight I was in a talkative mood.

Normally, we would travel north on the road in front of our house. Then we would swing back by the long way down our empty street. The long walk that night was filled with many questions about myself, my father, and my life in general. I asked Mama repeatedly about my father — about how he looked, and about the things he did. I could tell by her short answers and the way she was trying to change the subject that she was getting tired of answering me.

I asked her if she missed him, just like I had a hundred times before. Just then a tear came to her eye and she said, "More than you can imagine. Things would be different for us if your father hadn't died."

I asked her, "How?"

She said, "For one thing, when your father was alive, we didn't struggle as much. He always made sure we had food on our table. He made sure we had clothes and other things we needed. He was a hard worker, a good husband, and a good father."

Another tear started to roll down Mama's face as she said, "I wish he was alive. I loved him so much." At that point I wished I hadn't asked about my father at all, because it just seemed to make her upset.

As we strolled down the dirt road, she grasped my hand and said, "I love you, Maria." I squeezed her hand and said, "I love you, too. Don't worry, Mama. I'll get work tomorrow at the farm and we will have plenty of money for food."

She gave me a half-smile and said, "I know you will, dear."

By then we were nearly back home. As we approached our house, she said, "I want you to get right to bed. If you do get work at the farm tomorrow, you'll need to be well rested."

I couldn't help thinking what tomorrow might bring. Would it be a good day working at the farm? Would Mama get work at the market? Would we have a good meal for dinner tomorrow? Would Mama come home early and be happy? These thoughts and others rushed through my head with great anxiety, similar to the bad feeling that you get when you have a nightmare in the middle of the night.

Usually it was more difficult falling asleep in the summer, because the heat was sometimes unbearable, and our walls were so thin that our house didn't stay cool. Sometimes I would roll around for two or three hours before I could get to sleep. That night, my body was limp from exhaustion from the long troubling day I had, but I just couldn't get comfortable. So I lay in bed thinking of what tomorrow might bring.

— 2 —

The next thing I knew, I woke up to the sound of my mother bustling around the house. I turned over and looked up and saw her standing over me, saying, "Good morning, Maria. Get up and let's get going. Let's make this a great day."

Mama was usually happy in the morning, and today she seemed happier than I had seen her in a long time. I asked her what was going on. She said, "One of the farm workers came by and said that if you get down there early enough, there will be work for you today. Maybe our luck is changing, so hurry and get ready."

I hustled out of bed, hurried to my closet, and picked out a work outfit. I chose an old pair of faded blue jeans that had holes in both knees and a green shirt that had seen better days. I knew it would be scorching hot at the farm, so I didn't want to wear anything heavy. If I got an early start, it wouldn't be quite as bad, though.

I dressed quickly with much anticipation about what the day would bring. I hoped there would be plenty of work for my mother and I. If we had a good day, we would have a big meal at night. As I approached the table to eat breakfast, Mama said, "When you leave for the farm, I'm going to leave for the market and get an early start. I'm hoping I'll have a good day there and make us a good dinner."

I gobbled down my crackers and fruit. Mama said, "I packed you a lunch. You have an orange, some crackers, and some peanut butter. Eat it slow and make it last. I know you'll be hungry from all the hard work at the farm."

I didn't mind having a small lunch because sometimes I could trade with other workers and end up with more food than I originally had. Usually the workers would give me a piece of fruit or some bread to eat during the day. Sometimes they would even share their lunch with me.

I gave Mama a kiss and started toward the door when she said, "Maria, I'll be home early today. Have a good day and do a good job."

I told her goodbye as I walked through the door and started my journey toward the farm.

I was in an unusually good mood because I knew there was work for me. As I walked, I felt excited and thrilled, wondering what the day would bring. I didn't really mind that much that we didn't have a lot of extra fancy things. I just wanted my mother to be happy. I could not stand seeing her discouraged or disappointed when things didn't go well, and lately it seemed like more things were going wrong than right.

The long walk to the farm that day seemed shorter than usual. I couldn't wait to get started working. It was about 7:15 when I started walking to the farm and I arrived about an hour later, slightly covered in dirt from the dusty road. I didn't mind, because I figured I was going to get dirty working anyway.

My stomach was a little tight from the anticipation. As I approached Jesse, the farm leader, he looked up and said, "It's about time you got here, Maria. We can use you down at the barn."

A big smile spread across my face because the barn was my favorite place to work. I said, "All right, sir, right away." In the barn, I did things like clean the animals' pens, feed and brush the animals, milk the cows, and any other things that needed to be done.

Working in the barn was dirty, hard work, but I enjoyed it because I loved animals. It was a chance for me to spend time with them and forget about everything else. Plus, if you worked in the barn, you weren't out in the scorching sun all day. It was very hot in the barn, but it still wasn't as draining as being out in the unrelenting sun.

I hurried toward the barn to let Jesse know I was ready to get started. I didn't want him to change his mind and put me out in the fields. Labor in the fields was hard and never-ending. By the end of the day you could barely walk home from exhaustion.

I thought to myself that maybe this was going to be a great day. My mother had gone to the market early, and she had said she would be home early. I had gotten one of the better jobs at the farm. I would make enough money during the day to help Mama out a little.

Most of my summers were spent working, or at least trying to find work. I didn't mind because my mother was a good, hard-working person and she needed my help.

I looked up and saw the large, weathered, green wooden barn that symbolized an honest day's work for me. I was going to earn money that day and it felt good.

The barn actually had five buildings connected together. The front stables held approximately thirty horses. Presently, they only had twenty-two working and riding horses total. Toward the middle of the barn was an area that held about thirty cows. I wasn't sure how many there were, but it seemed like hundreds.

Toward the back of the barn, in smaller pens, were the pigs. They were in one of the older sections of the barn, which was noticeably different. The ceilings in the older section were much lower than in the newer section. The pens looked worn and showed many years of use.

In the back of the barn were all the goats and sheep. Outside, about forty feet away near the back of the barn, was a yellow-painted, worn chicken coop. Next to the chicken coop was a turkey pen that looked like it had not been painted in thirty years.

Even though the barn area was worn and tattered, it was a welcome sight. As I entered the barn, the head worker, Sam, approached me. He was a tall, lanky man with brown overalls. One of his front teeth was missing, which was clearly noticeable. It was funny. When he spoke and used the letter "s," he had a whistle in his voice because of that missing tooth.

Sam said, "All right, Maria. Let's get to work. I want you to take the cows one by one to the milking area. There are people waiting there now for them."

It wasn't difficult to take the cows to the milking area because they knew the way and they wanted to get milked. Just before the milking area was a narrow path about fifty feet away. It was railed in so the cows had no choice but to proceed that way.

The milking area was about seventy feet long by eighty feet wide and it had six automatic milking machines in it. It didn't take long for the cows to be milked. After about five minutes, you would take the same cow right back to where she was before.

After all the cows were milked, Sam told Angelina and me that he wanted all of the horses stables cleaned right away. Angelina was a thirteen-year-old girl that I liked very much. She was tall, skinny, and had messy, dark, straight hair. She was a good worker and I knew she would do a good job with me. We started right away.

All twenty-two stables needed to be cleaned. With two of us, it would take about an hour and a half. We would take a horse to a clean stable while we cleaned the dirty stable. Then we would take that horse back to his stable after we were done. We would have to clean up all the horse manure, put in fresh hay, and make sure there was fresh water and food. After that, we would brush the horse. It wasn't that difficult, but it was a very dirty, messy job. Even so, I enjoyed being around the horses very much.

After we were done with the horses, Sam approached us and said, "Come on, girls. You know the routine. Get cracking! The goat and sheep pens are next."

As I started toward the goat and sheep pens, I looked back and saw Sam looking in the horses' stables, inspecting our work. If the work wasn't up to his approval, he would always say, "I'm not paying for this kind of work. You get back in there and clean them right."

I had cleaned enough stables at the farm to know exactly what needed to be done. Sam almost always approved of my work. I do remember one time, though, when I first started cleaning the stables, when I forgot to put enough hay in the pens. Sam yelled at me and docked my pay. Lately I had not made any mistakes of that magnitude.

The sheep and goat pens were much easier to clean, even though there were many more pens than there were stables. It took about three hours for Angelina and I to finish the entire task. Angelina was not as proficient as I was with the animals' pens, but she tried very hard. After we were done with the goat and sheep pens, Sam came in to inspect our work.

Sam was a stern man who did not take any excuses when things were not done properly. He examined all the pens thoroughly, then he looked up at us, gave us a nod of approval, and said, "You have five minutes rest time before you start on the chicken coops." Five minutes was just enough time to gobble down a snack, get a drink of water, and get back to work.

Today was turning out to be a very busy day. I did not mind the hard work with very little time for breaks, because it made time go by much more quickly. The one bad thing about working straight through was that I was not able to trade food with the rest of the workers when they took their breaks. I was disappointed, because I depended on trading food with the other children. It was my favorite part of the day. I almost always ended up with more food than I had before.

I was a shrewd trader and bargained relentlessly. I bargained in a way that sparked the other workers' curiosity. I used their curiosity against them to make them give up their food. One thing I learned about trading was that you never traded on the first offer unless it was a tremendous deal. Another thing I learned was that you never showed a strong interest in any item.

This made the other children anxious and curious about what I would really trade for. If I really wanted something that someone had, I would divert their attention away from it by asking another person what they had. This would leave the person I was bargaining with in bewilderment. After they were confused, I would make an offer on an item that they had. Then I would usually get what I wanted at a good price. Sometimes the farm workers would give me something special like an apple or an orange out of the pure kindness of their hearts.

That five minute break would have to do. There was no way I was going to tell Sam that I needed to take a break after he had said we needed to get this work finished. After I took a long drink and ate my crackers and fruit, Angelina and I started toward the chicken coop. We knew exactly what needed to be done: clean the floor, check for any new eggs, clean the feeding trough, fill it up with food and water, and count and report to Sam how many chickens there were.

This took us approximately an hour. We had been at the farm for six hours and we still had the pigs and the other animals to contend with. After we were done with the chickens, we proceeded to the pig pens and started to clean them. By this time, the workers from the fields returned. Sam barked out a command to three of the field workers to get to the barn and help us with the rest of the animals. With five of us, the work went quickly.

In another hour and a half we were finished. I had already been on the farm for a total of almost eight hours. After a long day of work, I would always feel tired and achy, but the one good thing about the farm was that they had a shower that all the workers could use when they were done.

The showers were partitioned off and made of wood. The walls were old and discolored from long years of moisture penetrating them. A small pipelike nozzle hung over your head with a rope on it, which you would pull to make the water squirt out. After a long day in the barn a person would reek of manure and body odor. The shower was a welcome perk that almost everyone took advantage of.

After drying off and dressing, the workers would all get together and talk about what they were going to do with their pay. For an eight-hour work day I would receive approximately two hundred pesos, which would be equivalent to fifteen American dollars.

Each farm leader was responsible for distributing the money to his workers. Sam took about twenty minutes to come down with our pay. While I waited, I tried trading my peanut butter to a boy for some other food items. Almost all the other children had already eaten everything they had brought.

I was very tired and the temperature was over 100 degrees. While I waited for my pay, I sat quietly and finished what lunch I had left. When Sam approached me, he smiled and said, "You did a good job, Maria." He handed me two hundred pesos and two apples. My face lit up with excitement as he handed me the apples. I knew that was something extra that he didn't have to give me.

I tucked the money in my pants pocket and put one apple in the other pocket. I began to chomp one of the apples wildly right after I thanked Sam. The other apple I was going to save for my mother, who had probably put in an equally difficult day at the market.

I began to start walking home when Angelina came up to me and asked, "Did you get your pay?"

I said, "Yes."

She said, "Sam gave me two hundred pesos and an apple."

I said, "You must feel lucky."

She said, "Yes, I do."

I felt really good about myself, knowing Sam gave me an extra apple for the hard work I did. Even though I didn't mention the extra apple to Angelina, somehow I think she knew that Sam had done something special for me, too.

The long, tedious walk back home was no different than any other day. The heat was sweltering. My feet were throbbing from the long day in the barn. My clothes were already very dirty and smelly from cleaning all the pens, and dusty from the road, but the rinse down I took earlier helped.

Even though the muscles in my arms and lower back were aching, I knew I would have to go down to the well and draw water. When I got home, I would have to wash my clothes and do my normal chores. I thought about all the stories I had heard about the children in the United States. I heard they lived in big houses with refrigerators, televisions, and their own bedrooms.

I thought to myself, how great it would be if we had a lot of money. Then I wouldn't have to go to work every day.

I could spend my summers playing. I wouldn't have to worry about not having any food to eat.

As I approached my house, Mama met me at the door with a smile and asked, "How are you, honey?"

I said, "Fine, but I'm very tired. I cleaned the animals' pens today."

Mama knew that cleaning the animals' pens was not one of the hardest jobs on the farm, but she knew I would still feel achy and tired.

I asked her how she did at the market. She gave me a slight frown and said, "Not very well. I managed to earn enough money for some milk, a loaf of bread, and a jar of peanut butter."

Just then, I pulled the apple that I had saved for her out of my pocket, and handed her the two hundred pesos. Her eyes started to water a little. She gave me a big hug and said, "I love you." While she was hugging me she said, "You keep the apple, honey."

I told her I had eaten one on the way home and that one was for her.

She said, "I'll tell you what, Maria. We'll split it at dinner time."

I just nodded and said, "I have to do the laundry because my clothes are filthy."

Mama told me she would do the laundry for me and to go wash up and rest before dinner. I said, "Thank you," and went inside the house and changed out of my dirty clothes. I ended up lying down and actually falling asleep. I woke to the sight of my mother standing over the couch I slept on, saying, "Maria, it's time for dinner." As I sluggishly rolled off the couch, I rubbed my eyes, looked up, and saw a beautiful blue vase sitting on the table, with an orange sitting next to it.

I asked Mama, "Where did you get those things?"

She said, "Someone gave me the vase and I bought the orange."

As I set the table, I noticed that we were having peanut butter sandwiches, milk, an orange, and an apple for dinner. We had a whole loaf of bread, which was a surprise. I thought that was a good quantity of food considering she said she'd had a poor day at the market.

The great thing was that we still had the money left that I earned at the farm. I knew that it would have to be used for food or for whatever else we needed. That night I had three peanut butter sandwiches, half an apple, half an orange, and a glass of milk for dinner. I remember feeling very satisfied after that meal.

Mama helped me clean the table that night. She also helped me do the dishes, as she often did when I'd had a long, tedious day. I felt a little sore and tired, so I asked her if we could skip our walk that night. She said yes, and that we would just stay home and read.

I had a small assortment of books that Mama had gotten from people she knew at the market. My favorite book was *Anne of Green Gables*.

Reading helped me escape from most of my problems. I could read a book and forget about almost anything. I used to see myself as one of the characters. I would imagine what I would do if I was in the same situation. Even though I only had about twenty books, I would read them over and over again. I enjoyed them very much.

I dreamed of owning my own farm one day. On my farm I would have horses and pigs. I would also have an enormous plot of land where I could grow corn, wheat, and all different kinds of fruit. I enjoyed envisioning how things would be much better when I grew up.

That night I read for an hour. After that, Mama and I talked for about thirty minutes before I got ready for bed. I was very tired that night and I knew that I would sleep well. I hoped there would be work tomorrow at the farm. I also hoped that my mother would have an excellent day at the market.

I always prayed every night before I went to bed. The last thing I remembered that night was me asking God to watch over my mother and myself and to keep us safe.

— 3 —

Morning came quickly. I slept so soundly that I did-
n't remember a thing. Usually I would wake up
once or twice during the night and roll over and go
back to sleep, but that night was different. I woke slowly to
the sound of Mama getting ready. She was preparing for her
day at the market. She saw that I was lying awake, so she
said, "Come on, let's get moving."

I loved the safe, comfortable feeling I had when I was
lying on that old couch. I felt like no matter how bad my
day may have been, as long as I had my couch to escape to,
I would be fine.

As I got up, I thought about playing soccer with my
friends. A smile immediately came to my face. I thought
about José and how much fun we had together. We loved to
kick the soccer ball around. I asked Mama if I could play

with my friends today after the farm. She hesitated and said, "It depends on how my day goes at the market."

She knew if she said yes, she would have to do most of my chores after work. Normally, she would do this so I wouldn't miss out on playing with my friends. But usually after a long day at the farm, I just wanted to rest and didn't feel like running around anyway.

I was in a big hurry that morning because I needed to be at the farm early to get work. I ate a peanut butter sandwich and drank a glass of milk for breakfast. I packed ten crackers, a lump of peanut butter, and an apple for my lunch.

I hoped that the peanut butter would net me a nice trade that day. Sometimes a boy named Roberto would trade beef jerky for almost anything. His dad smoked his own meat at home and he always had plenty extra. Meat sounded really delicious to me because I rarely had it. Once in a while I would trade for enough beef jerky to bring some home. But I wasn't even sure if I was going to be working that day or if I would see Roberto at all. It all depended on what work had to do be done that day.

After I got ready, Mama said, "I love you" and I was on my way. I felt pretty good on the way to the farm. I had some nice thoughts about when I grew up and how my mother would come live in my mansion with me. The dirt-covered road didn't even bother me that day. I was so deep in thought I hardly noticed the dust clouds blowing about.

When I arrived at the farm, Sam said, "Sorry, there is no work today. Check back tomorrow."

The walk back was less than pleasurable. My dreams of owning a mansion turned into thoughts of whether we would ever have a steady income.

I hurried home because I knew I had many chores to catch up on. I had the laundry to do. I had to clean dishes, and I had to get water from the well. The heat of the day had not yet reached its full intensity, but I already felt drained from the long day I'd had yesterday. The temperature was about 88 degrees, which felt much hotter because I walked at such a rapid pace.

The first thing I did when I got back home was to put my lunch away. I did all my chores after that, in about three hours. When I was done it was about 2:00. Then I ate lunch and remembered the pleasant thoughts I'd had when I woke up about playing soccer. I rushed over to José's house to see if he could come out and play, but he was already gone.

When it was very hot out, we never played soccer for long. I knew I didn't have much time before my friends would be quitting. I hurried over to where we normally played. I saw most of the kids from our neighborhood there. I asked if I could join in. José said, "Where were you? We've been here for an hour."

I told José that I had my chores to do first. I said, "My mother will not let me play until they are done."

José said, "You are on our team. We are losing three to two and we could use you."

That afternoon went by quickly, as it always did when we were playing soccer. Before I knew it, it was 4:30 and everyone was breaking up to go home for dinner. I didn't know when my mother would be home that day, so I took my time getting back.

When I got home at 5:30, Mama was just getting home too. I had an idea about the type of day she'd had because of the frustrated look on her face. When I asked her how things went, she said, "No matter how hard I tried, I just couldn't make any money. Life is like that sometimes."

I told her that I had gotten there early, but there was not any work at the farm, either. Mama looked unhappy, but said, "I do have a pound of bacon, three pears, a loaf of bread, and a small bag of carrots. I used the money that you made at the farm yesterday, as well as the small amount that I made today. And we still have some peanut butter from yesterday left over, so we will be fine."

After dinner that night, Antonio stopped over for a visit. He was a very handsome man and was only about thirty years old. He was about five feet, ten inches tall, with short dark hair and a dark complexion. He had warm, charming, brown eyes, a very muscular build, and a strong demeanor.

Upon his arrival, we immediately knew something was wrong by the concerned look on his face. We asked him if there was anything bothering him, but he just said, "No."

He always brought us something when he came to visit. This time he brought us two towels, a blanket, a bag of apples, a gallon of milk, three jars of peanut butter, a candy bar, seven bananas, and a cup and a saucer.

I screeched when I saw all the wonderful gifts he brought us. I asked him, "What's going on? Is it Christmas?"

He said, "No, but I do have something to talk to you about." We went inside, sat down, and waited for him to start.

Antonio started by saying, "Anita and Maria, you know I was very close friends with Miguel. I've always been around to help you whenever you needed me. I lost my job as a carpenter because of the lack of work around here and

I have been looking for another one. Well, I found one in Mexico City and I'll be leaving at the end of the week. I'll try to come back two or three times a year to visit you. And I will try to send a little money, a few times a year, or when I can."

Both my mother's and my mouth just dropped. We knew we could always count on Antonio if we were in a jam. A feeling of sorrow rushed over me and I actually felt frightened. Without him here, things would be much more difficult for us. I felt like I was being abandoned. I felt like I was going to lose a close friend.

Just then Antonio said, "Now come on. Drop the long faces. I'll be back when I can." But I knew, deep in my heart, this was never going to happen. Mexico City was so far away. It would be almost impossible for him to break away and come see us.

That night was very special. We sat and talked about so many fond memories, everything from my father, to when I was born, to when I first walked. I didn't want it to end. I felt like the thoughts and memories from that night would stay with me for the rest of my life. It was one of the few times growing up that I could remember when the night just seemed electric. Antonio was a very special person in our modest lives and I knew things were definitely not going to be the same without him. He ended up staying until 10:30, which was considered very late for us.

The next morning came all too fast. When I woke, I was confused and unsure how to feel. One part of me felt happy because of the great time we had last night, while another part of me felt empty and lost because our good friend Antonio was going to move away.

As Mama came in the room, I thought she knew how I was feeling. She said, "Antonio has been a very special friend of ours. Even though we're discouraged that he's leaving, we still need to go on with our lives as he would expect us to. He told us he would come back and visit us. I have known Antonio for a long time and he always keeps his word. So I believe we will be seeing him again soon. Come on, Maria. Let's start our day."

That was one of the longest days I had in a long time. There was no work at the farm. I completed all of my chores early. I had three free hours in the afternoon to do whatever I wanted, but I didn't feel much like playing soccer because I felt so empty. Our friend Antonio was moving and I felt terrible. I remembered all the good times we'd had when Antonio was around and I was hurting.

When Mama came home around 5:00, right when I saw her, I began to cry. She came to me and asked, "Are you all right?"

I said, "There was no work at the farm today. I was home all day alone." I told her I had done my chores and was very depressed about Antonio leaving. Mama grabbed me, gave me a hug, and said, "We have had a great friend in Antonio. He will always be our friend, no matter where he is."

I asked her, "How are we going to get food when we don't have any money?"

She said, "I had a good day at the market today, and besides, Antonio gave us so much food that it will last for quite some time. So don't worry about anything."

I felt much better after talking to Mama. I was just lonely that day and felt very empty inside. She had cheered me up considerably. We had a great meal that night to ease our sadness. We had ham, apples, peanut butter, bread, and milk. I even had a rare candy bar for dessert. I thought, *Wow, what a meal!* After dinner, Mama told me that Antonio was going to come and see us before he left on Friday. It was Wednesday night, just two days before he was going to leave. I couldn't wait to see him again.

Mama gave me some reassuring words just before bed. She said, "We have always done well with me working at the market and with you at the farm. We have always provided food for each other. The fact that Antonio will be in Mexico City just means that we will have to work a little harder." I felt a little better with her comforting me that night. I thought that maybe things would be fine after all.

The next morning I woke up feeling much more confident. I felt happy to be alive and was ready to start my day. Somehow, I felt that things would work out.

Thursday went by rapidly because the farm had work for me that day. I spent most of the day in the fields helping pick apples. After the dusty walk home, my mother was waiting for me. She said, "I had a bad day at the market. It is fine, though, because we have plenty of leftover food from yesterday. And besides, Antonio will be over tomorrow morning."

Mama was very quiet at dinner that evening. I asked her if everything was all right. She said, "Yes," then added that she was also a little depressed because Antonio was leaving. She said, "I just don't know if I could have made it when your father died if Antonio hadn't been here. Antonio is a fine man and he always did what was best for us. He was a real blessing when we needed help the most. I'm going to miss him so much."

That evening we went for a long walk. I could tell by the look on Mama's face that she was distant and distressed. I wanted to believe that it was because she would miss Antonio. I didn't want to believe it was because we needed him for survival.

When we got home, Mama said, "Antonio will be over first thing in the morning to say goodbye."

I had a difficult time getting to sleep that night. I was very distraught and even had a nauseated feeling in my stomach. I hoped Antonio would change his mind and stay here with us.

The next morning I woke to my mother saying, "Wake up. Antonio is here." When I jumped out of bed, I felt rushed and unready for his departure. I got dressed faster than I ever had before.

When I finally went outside, Antonio was standing there hugging my mother and saying goodbye. Mama had tears rolling down her cheeks. Antonio turned to me, gave me a hug and a kiss on the top of my head, and said, "I'll miss you, Maria. I have something very special for you."

He pulled a six pack of Hershey candy bars out of his bag and said, "I'll always remember your special smile. I will never forget all the incredible times that we had together. You and your mother mean so much to me. I'm sorry I have to move. I'll be back to visit you soon. After all, how can I stay away from my favorite people in the whole world?"

By this time I was crying profusely. I felt absolutely horrible! Somehow I knew Antonio probably would not be back for quite a while. He had to be struggling because he had lost his job over a month ago. Before he lost his job, he barely made ends meet. I knew this from overhearing many conversations between my mother and him. I knew he was not a wealthy man by any means. He was always there for us, though. Now he was leaving and we would have to fend for ourselves.

He said his last goodbyes and I watched him drive away. A feeling of hopelessness that seemed unshakable came over me. I couldn't help but wonder if that was the last time I would ever see our good friend Antonio.

— 4 —

An hour later, when my tears dried, things seemed to be somber, but normal. The fact that Antonio was gone was a difficult thing to overcome. Mama said, "Sometimes the anticipation of an event is worse than the event itself. And there is nothing left to do but go on with our lives."

The walk to the farm that day was a long, troubled one. Thoughts of how we were going to make it without Antonio ran through my head repeatedly. I barely thought of the dust that engulfed the road. I just wanted to get busy and forget about all my problems.

Unfortunately, there wasn't any work at the farm that day. The long walk home seemed to be worse than usual, because I felt disgruntled and disappointed. The penetrating heat and never-ending dust just contributed to my misery.

When I returned home, I finished my chores and went to see if José wanted to play soccer. Unfortunately, José wasn't home. I found out that he was gone for a week to his grandmother's house ten miles away. I couldn't help thinking that everything just kept getting worse and worse.

I waited for my mother impatiently, feeling a little frustrated with my life. But by the time Mama eventually got home, I felt a little better. That night we had a nice meal and then talked about school. Mama said, "School will be starting in three weeks, so we must be prepared." I always felt a little nervous about going back to school.

The next three weeks flew by. Work at the farm was scarce and my mother had equally poor luck at the market. We had enough food to last us, though, because Antonio left us a sizable amount before he left. We seemed to be getting by without Antonio there, but I had no idea what the future would bring.

Before I knew it, it was the night before the first day of school. As I said my prayers that night, I prayed that one day Mama would find a better job, and that I would be able to help her out with money and food when I got older. I felt a little selfish because I asked for so much for ourselves. That night I had trouble sleeping. It felt like I only slept for two good hours all night.

The next morning I sprang out of bed in a fury. The sun had just barely come up when I was moving about. I wanted to get to school early enough to get a good seat. I also wanted to make a good impression on my teacher before the busy day started. I hoped seventh grade would be fun like sixth grade had been. I was concerned about my teacher, though. I had found out a week earlier that I had Mrs. Hernandez, who had a reputation of being very strict. Even though I was a fairly good student, I still was concerned. The first day of school always brought a certain amount of anxiety for me.

I hadn't gotten any new clothes for school yet, so Mama told me to get out my best outfit. She said, "I'll try to get you something at the market this week."

I slowly went through my clothes and picked out a pair of old faded jeans. They were light blue in color and didn't have a single hole in them. The bottoms were frayed a bit, but they still looked decent. They were an inch too short because I grew so much over the last six months. The jeans weren't perfect, but I liked them. I also picked out a light pink shirt that I wore a lot last spring. The shirt looked somewhat faded, but was very presentable.

As I left for school at 7:30 that morning, Mama said, "Remember, you get hot lunch every day this year." The school had a program for low income families that allowed me to receive a free lunch daily. We always believed that everyone should provide for themselves., but Mama said that this was different. I knew Mama was very happy about me receiving a free lunch, since without my working at the farm, money would be very tight. At least I would be getting one solid meal during the day.

So many thoughts were rushing through my head that morning that I was almost late leaving for school. José and I would always walk to school together every day. We would meet down at the end of my street.

On the way to school, José and I talked about how we had fun at recess and how school was sort of fun at times. One funny thing about José was that he never took his soccer ball to school. He claimed he didn't want to ruin it, or for it to get stolen.

The thirty-minute walk went by so rapidly that day. The next thing I knew, we were standing right in front of our school. It was a faded, yellow aluminum building with old wooden windows and a large flagpole in front of it that flew the Mexican flag.

The outside had a large playground with an old rusted slide and a four-person swing-set with rubber swings. Over on the other side of the school was a field where we played baseball, soccer, cricket, or whatever game the teacher decided on.

The school taught grades K-12. About two hundred students attended Hanco School. Some classes had up to forty students in them and were quite crowded. I hoped our class would be small so I could get help easily if I needed it. Some classes were split classes, where two and sometimes three different grades were represented. You could have a fifth grader in your seventh grade class and not even think twice about it.

The classrooms were about thirty feet square and held a maximum of forty students. The space you were assigned to work in was small, which forced students to work efficiently. The blackboards were small and shabby from the many years of use. The classrooms were decorated with pictures from around the world. Above the blackboard was written, "You can go anywhere and be anything you want to be if you work hard enough."

The first time I saw that statement above the blackboard, I thought to myself that I was going to live in the United States one day. I would have a large house like the ones I heard about in so many stories. I made an agreement with my inner self that I would do this, no matter what. I didn't want to live in a small shack the rest of my life. I was determined and I would not settle for anything less.

Seeing my mother struggle day in and day out just motivated me more. I respected Mama for all she had done for me, but I didn't want to live wondering where our next meal would come from. I knew that our struggling was beyond Mama's control. It was because we lived in rural Mexico where there were not many jobs.

That morning went well. I was able to read to a child from another class because we had a program called Reading Buddies. A student from kindergarten or first grade would be assigned to a seventh grade student. At Reading Buddies time, you would go to their classroom, pick a book, and help the student learn to read it. It was a chance for us to get out of our classroom for twenty minutes or so. It also gave a child a chance to learn to read one-on-one with a mentor. It was extremely effective in helping the younger children learn to read.

I remembered that day specifically because it was the first day of school and the first time I met Elena, my Reading Buddy. She was five years old and as cute as a button, with long black hair, clear dark skin, and beautiful deep brown eyes. She appeared shy and talked with a soft voice.

I remember when I first saw her. I walked with her to the bookcase as I introduced myself to her. I said, "Hello, my name is Maria. What's yours?"

She tilted her head down and mumbled, "Elena."

I said, "Elena, what a nice name."

She smiled and said, "Thank you."

I thought to myself, *What a polite little girl for being just five years old.* I asked if she would pick out the first book, and she nodded and chose a book called *Who Am I?*

The book gave hints about what a person did for a living. One page stated, "I help people when they are sick. I give them medicine to make them feel better." Obviously that was a doctor. Elena guessed them all right. I was very impressed.

I absolutely loved little children. I sometimes wished I had a little sister or brother. I knew it was hard enough for my mother with just me, though. I don't think she could have handled supporting one more child.

I wanted to have children someday. I hoped I could have three or four. I hoped we would have a beautiful house, and a yard with a swing-set and a grassy area to play soccer. My dreams were always vivid and I was determined to make them a reality.

After reading two books to my newfound friend, I said, "Goodbye. I'll see you again next week." She didn't know how to read yet, but the fact that I had an opportunity to help a child made me feel good inside. It took away some of the pain of not having a father and having to fight so hard to survive.

Mrs. Hernandez walked us all back to our classrooms so we could get back to work. We didn't have much time to sit around in class because Mrs. Hernandez would always know if you were not paying attention. I knew this from talking to her former students. Her reputation was that she was strict, but fair. She felt you were there to learn, period.

As the day went by, I realized that we would be doing more math this year. Math was not one of my best subjects. I enjoyed reading, Spanish, and English the most. In our school, you were taught two languages from an early age, English and Spanish. The school believed that since we lived so close to the United States, we should know how to speak both languages. Although we spoke Spanish at home, I preferred to speak English because my dream was to live in a mansion in the United States some day.

School really flew by that first day, as it always did. The teacher always seemed to show us so many things that we didn't have time to be bored. Toward the end of the last hour, a thought flashed into my head about my mother. I wondered if she had done well at the market. I was hoping that we would have a big meal that night. I was hungry and couldn't wait to get home.

After school, many of the children would stay for an hour or so to play soccer. I almost never stayed after to play, because I always had homework and chores to do. Even when I went to school, things like laundry and dishes would still have to be done. It seemed like time was always short after school.

While some children were out with their friends playing soccer, I would be helping Mama with chores so she didn't have to do everything. I really didn't mind because she was so helpful to me. I am sure some mothers would give up in our situation. They wouldn't be able to cope with things and would just quit. Not my mother, though. She was a fighter. She always seemed to get us through whatever would happen.

The school bell was a welcome sound for all of us. It symbolized freedom that every student in the school could relate to. When I heard the bell that day, I felt elated. The bell actually made me feel that things would be terrific today.

I grabbed my things and went for the door when José asked me, "Can you stay and play soccer after school?"

I just grinned and said, "No, thank you. I have work at home to do."

José said, "Well, one day you'll be sorry that you didn't stay. One day I'm going to be a world famous soccer player. And when I am, people will come from all over the world to see me play."

I said, "Oh, come on, José. You have a long way to go before you get there."

He said, "Well, I'm going to do it and that's final."

I thought to myself as I walked out the door, *I guess everyone has their dreams of how they are going to get out of this poverty stricken area.* José's was soccer. I guess that was no different than the way I felt about moving to the United States.

The walk home felt longer than usual because I was so hungry. The free lunch program hadn't started yet, and I could feel the hunger pains in my stomach knotting away at my insides. I felt like I had an empty hole inside me. Finally, when I did arrive home, I ate some crackers and peanut butter, which really hit the spot. After that snack, I patiently waited for Mama to get home from work.

She arrived home about 5:30. I had been home from school for about two hours by then and most of the chores were done. I still had some laundry to pull off the line out back, and I had to fold and put all the clothes away.

I could tell by the look on Mama's face that she didn't have a very good day. She asked, "How was your first day of school?"

I replied, "It went well. I think it will be a little harder than last year." I told her about my Reading Buddy, which brought a bright smile to her face.

When I asked her about her day, she frowned and said, "It didn't go well. I spent most of the day there and didn't make much of anything. I was able to bring home only a loaf of bread and a banana."

I looked at her and said, "That's all right, because I ate a little after school. We still have a few carrots and half a jar of peanut butter left over."

I continued, "We will make the best of things. Things will be better tomorrow. You'll see." Always before, when things seemed to be at their worst, Antonio would stop by and bring our spirits up. Of course, now that Antonio had moved away to Mexico City, he wouldn't be showing up any time soon.

I asked Mama if she wanted me to go and try to get work at the farm tomorrow instead of going to school. She emphatically said, "No." She believed that it was crucial for me to go to school and learn as much as I could. She wanted me to earn a decent living when I got older. I knew she would never let me miss school anyway, unless it was an absolute emergency.

She gave me a half-hearted smile and said, "Things will turn around for us, don't worry." I couldn't help thinking to myself that we could be in trouble. We had no recourse with Antonio gone. We would have to face all of our problems head on.

Terrifying thoughts entered my head that evening. I couldn't shake them. I kept worrying if we would eat supper tomorrow, or if we would even make it another day in our house. Would I need to quit school and help my mother, or would we have to live in the streets? I was so filled with anxiety that I felt a little nauseated.

Before we ate, Mama said a long prayer for grace. We both felt a little better after we prayed. As we ate, my mother talked about how she felt that God would take care of us. She said, "He will always be there for us. I have a strong belief that things happen for a reason and that destiny will prevail."

Our walk went by rapidly that evening and before I knew it, we were back home. We spent the next thirty minutes looking through material I'd brought home about the seventh grade and looking at some of my books.

My schoolbooks were old and outdated. They had been used by many seventh graders before me. The copyright date was from eleven years previous. My teacher had told us, "It doesn't matter how old the books are, because things like math and history rarely change."

After we were done looking over my school information, we cleaned up and got ready for bed. Surprisingly, I wasn't hungry at all. The bread and peanut butter that we ate filled me up. I was feeling a little more confident about the future. I had no idea what the future would bring, but Mama made me feel like everything would fall into place.

— 5 —

The next morning was a difficult one. We woke up fifteen minutes late and I had to rush to get ready for school. It seemed so hectic that morning. I felt like I was a race horse approaching the starting gate. There wasn't much time for breakfast and there wasn't much food anyway, so I grabbed my things and scurried out the door. I walked at a fast pace because I didn't want to be late on my second day of school.

I was in a better mood that morning, thinking it would be a good day at the market for my mother. It was a flea market where peddlers would come and set up tables. They would sell and trade just about anything. I knew Mama worked for one of the vendors, helping her with her booths, and that she got paid mostly based on how much she sold. She also got paid a small amount even if she didn't sell anything. Mama seemed to enjoy working there and actually had done pretty well with it over the years.

When I arrived at school, all of the students were piling into their classrooms. I wasn't late; I was just on time. As I walked through the door, my stomach rumbled from a lack of breakfast.

As I scurried to my seat, the teacher reminded us we wouldn't be doing Reading Buddies that day. I felt a little down because that was the best part of the day. I worked feverishly all morning long on the assignments Mrs. Hernandez gave us.

As the morning progressed, I became extremely hungry. My stomach felt so empty I began to feel dizzy. I could feel the acid inside churning a little. Sometimes when I felt hungry, I would concentrate on school and take my mind off the fact that I had not eaten in a while. This time the feeling was barely tolerable.

The next hour went by slowly until lunchtime finally arrived. The school lunches were never particularly great, but when you are hungry anything tastes fabulous. Today was the first day of free lunches for me. Usually I got to eat enough so I would stay full most of the day.

My mother said that free lunches were important because she never had to worry about me going hungry at school. She also said that it was so much easier than trying to pack a lunch every day. Mama said, "It's a blessing that the school provides lunch for children who need it. So we should be thankful for it."

As I stood in line, I could smell the freshly cooked noodles that meant we were going to have spaghetti. Mrs. Concordia, our lunch monitor, usually would give me a big helping. Sometimes she would give me more than I could eat. I knew that Mrs. Concordia had talked to my mother and knew about our situation.

When I reached Mrs. Concordia, she smiled and said, "Hello, Maria. Your usual today, dear?"

I smiled and said, "Yes, please."

She gave me two big scoops of spaghetti, two rolls, one scoop of Jell-O, one container of milk, and one cookie. I was pleased to see all that food on my plate at once. I felt like that was enough food for a king.

I found a seat and took my first bite quickly, so I could get the strong taste of the spaghetti sauce in my mouth. I was like a child on Christmas morning, waiting to rip all her presents open right away. I felt like gobbling the entire plate of food down in one bite.

My friend Francesca came up and asked, "Can I sit next to you?"

I said, "Yes."

Francesca was a tall girl with dark hair, a large, protruding nose, and big, oversized feet. I liked Francesca. We ate lunch together on a regular basis. As she sat down, I said to her, "Good lunch. Wow!"

She took her first bite, smiled, and replied, "Yes, it is."

Francesca was in my class and also received free lunches at school. Her father was a car mechanic who didn't have steady work, and her mother cleaned house for a wealthy family forty miles away.

Francesca sometimes would come to school with bruises on her arms or legs. When I asked her about them, she would always reply, "I fell." Or she would say, "I bumped into something." She was clumsy and did have oversized feet, but I had my suspicions about her parents. I had never been to her house, so I didn't know what her parents were like, but she never invited anyone over, to my knowledge.

I had asked her to come to my house many times. She would always come up with the most unusual excuses. I remember one time when she said, "My father has a rich uncle coming to visit from the United States and I can't make it."

Another time she said, "My father is fixing a limousine and he needs me there to help with the tools." I had never even seen a limousine. I only knew what one looked like from pictures of a wedding I once saw. Even though I knew Francesca was making things up, I liked her anyway and considered her a close friend.

When I finished my lunch, I smiled at Francesca and said, "I'm very full!" My stomach had gone from being totally empty and growling to being stuffed. Lunchtime was the best part of my day.

I'd had a great meal and was ready to play outside on our break. We had fifteen minutes outside after lunch. Every day, almost everyone played soccer, except for a few girls that played on the old, battered playground equipment. I enjoyed recess immensely and I always had fun. I just loved to play soccer as much as I could, every day at school. It was my favorite thing to do.

The rest of the day went by quickly. Before I knew it, I was packing my things to go home. School always went better after lunch. I didn't bother to ask Francesca about playing after school because I knew what her reply would be.

The walk home was uneventful so my mind wandered. I thought about our friend Antonio in Mexico City. I also thought about Mama who was at work. I was still rather full from the meal at lunch, so I wasn't thinking of food. As I approached my front door, I remembered I would have chores to do after I did my homework. I had to fold some clothes and get water from the well.

By this time of year, late August, it was still very hot during the day. The temperatures reached near 100 degrees almost every day. The nights were cooling off a little better, though. My teacher said, "Your body adjusts to the long, hot summer." She claimed that your body could build up resistance to the heat over a period of time. She claimed we would adapt like an animal would. All I knew was that it wasn't as bad as it had been during early summer, when temperatures reached 115 degrees on occasion.

Mama came home late, around 6:00. As she came through the door she said, "It wasn't the greatest day for me. It was very slow at the market. I hardly made any money at all. All I brought home was a loaf of bread."

Now our cupboards were nearly empty. I told her that I was still very full from lunch, and I started to tell her about the spaghetti I had when she said, "I don't feel well. I just want to lie down."

I had never seen Mama like that before. She always would listen to me about my day. She must have been very frustrated or sick. So I went outside and began hanging up the laundry. Just then I heard crying. The walls in our house were not very thick and you could hear through them easily.

I stopped immediately and hurried toward the house. I wondered what had happened and what was wrong. As I approached her door, I could hear her persistent sobbing. I opened the door and asked, "Mama, what's wrong?"

She looked up with her eyes full of tears and said, "I had such a bad day and I feel bad for you that I didn't bring any food home. I'm so tired of living like this. You deserve so much more than this, and I miss your father. I wish he was here now."

I walked up to her, gave her a hug, and said, "It's all right." I told her that I ate so much at school that day, I thought I was going to burst. I said that I was really happy and that we should be thankful for what we have. I told her that I missed Papa too.

Apparently, Mama felt somewhat comforted by the fact that I ate well at school. She seemed content and began to settle down. Even so, I felt uneasy the entire evening.

I asked Mama if she wanted to take a walk and she said, "Yes." So we went on our nightly walk together, trying to put our troubles behind us. Words were a little hard to come by as we strolled on our usual route. I tried mentioning how school was and that my friend Francesca seemed to be doing well, but Mama seemed preoccupied and didn't want to talk.

My mother knew of Francesca's problems. She knew she came to school bruised sometimes, and she suspected her father of abuse. Mama once went so far as to complain to the school about it, but her complaint didn't help. Around here, people tend to mind their own business. A few bruises now and then on a twelve-year-old aren't going to spark much attention.

As we completed our leisurely walk, Mama said, "I'm going to try really hard at the market tomorrow. Things have to get better." There was something about her that night that worried me, but I didn't know what it was. I just felt uneasy after our walk.

I had never seen my mother get as upset as she did that night. I felt as if she had lost all of her confidence or belief in herself. I grabbed Mama's hand and said, "I think you are going to do great at the market tomorrow!" Then I smiled at her.

As she smiled back she said, "I'm sure I will."

— 6 —

I got up much earlier the next morning because I didn't like the rushed feeling I'd had the morning before. My mother always told me that being late was a bad habit and that I should always be on time. She said, "Most people could be tremendous students or anything they wanted, but some people just can't be on time."

Mama always taught me that being punctual was very important. She claimed that people who were constantly late all the time were unprepared, or they just didn't care. So my goal for the school year was that I was going to be on time as much as I could.

There was very little food for breakfast that morning. I knew Mama must have been hungry that morning because she hadn't had dinner the night before. She always made sure I would have food to eat before her. I was hungry, but I just ate a little and saved the rest for her. We had eleven crackers, two carrots, and a small amount of peanut butter left.

I told Mama I wasn't hungry, even though we skipped dinner yesterday. I told her I would get a huge lunch at school. I smiled at her and told her I had to get going. As I was completing my ritual of gathering my things before school, she said, "I'm probably going to stay late at the market. I need to try to get whatever work I can. We need the extra money."

I just smiled and said, "That's fine." I had a feeling this was going to be a better day. I just knew it. When I hustled to school that morning, I remembered it was Reading Buddies day. This thought brought me instant pleasure.

School was uneventful. I enjoyed eating my usual huge meal at lunch. I had macaroni and cheese, apple slices, bread, milk, and a brownie. I was very full again, thanks to Mrs. Concordia.

Things went much better that day. I was in a rather jovial mood after school. I kept thinking things were going to get better for us. I kept thinking my mother's day must have been better as well.

She arrived home much later than normal, around 7:00, and seemed very ornery and crabby. Things didn't go well at the market again for her.

She said she had earned very little money and had nothing for us but a loaf of bread. I explained that I'd had a big lunch and I was still full. She didn't seem to be moved by my statement at all. She just had a distant look in her eyes.

That loaf of bread would have to last us for dinner and breakfast. I only ate one medium sized piece for dinner. That night at home was one of the most quiet, somber nights I remember. We even skipped our walk, and I went to bed early because all of my chores were done.

The next day was Thursday, and I was already looking forward to the weekend. No school on the weekend meant possible work at the farm. On Saturdays during the school year, I would work at the farm to obtain a little extra money. Work was scarce that time of year, but now and then I would get lucky and get work. I would probably spend time with my mother on Sunday. She very rarely did much on Sunday, because she always said it was a family day. On Sunday we would walk two miles to church and spend two hours at the service. I liked Sunday service because it was a time when everyone sang and was in a good mood.

I started school that Thursday like any other day. At lunch I had another typical meal: a large plate of stew, two oranges, two rolls, and a cupcake.

When I returned to class, I remember thinking to myself that I was lucky. If I didn't get those free meals at lunch, I would have been hungry all the time.

What happened next was something I could never have prepared myself for. The principal, Mr. Ricardo, came down to my classroom and asked to speak with Mrs. Hernandez privately. She told us to get out our math books and start looking over our assignment.

She came back about five minutes later with an absolutely dreadful look on her face. She came over to me and said, "Maria, can you gather your things and come with me?"

At this point my heart was racing with concern. I asked her if something was wrong, or if I had done something wrong and was going to be punished.

She said, "No, dear. We are just going down to the principal's office for a moment." I knew that something had to be wrong, because I had never been asked to go to the principal's office with all my things before.

As I walked down the hall, a feeling of fear penetrated my body. I remember thinking that I must be in big trouble as I was meekly escorted to the office. Thoughts kept popping into my head — did something happen to my mother? Was I in trouble for something I did? Was I going home early for some reason? I just couldn't shake the feeling that something bad was about to happen.

When I entered Principal Ricardo's office, there were two men waiting for me. One man was bald, short, and had very dark skin. He wore a blue suit with brown shoes and looked a little chubby. The other man had dark hair with a thick mustache. He was tall, thin, and had on a brown suit with a light brown vest.

Principal Ricardo said, "Sit down, Maria." At this point, I was so nervous, I could barely breathe or talk. My stomach felt like there was a hive of bees in it, buzzing around. I felt like I was going to throw up right there.

Principal Ricardo introduced the two men as Detective Gonzales and Detective Nuevo. He said, "These two men need to speak with you."

The detectives started to ask questions like, "Does your mother have a lot of things at home that seem unusual?" Puzzled, I said, "No." They asked me if she always had extra money. I said "no" again, then I asked, "What is this about?"

The detectives looked at each other. Detective Nuevo said, "Your mother was caught stealing at the market today. She was caught trying to steal 17,000 pesos."

My heart raced and felt like it was going to hit the floor. How could this be true? My mother was one of the most honest people in the world. She wouldn't even take a cracker that didn't belong to her. I shouted, "No! That isn't true. My mother is honest and hard-working!"

Detective Gonzales said, "She was caught red-handed and she is in a lot of trouble. Everyone at the market said she was a hard worker. They said they couldn't believe it either. But it is true, Maria. She has to be charged with larceny."

The detectives went on to explain what the details were. Detective Nuevo said, "Apparently, your mother went in where the cash box was kept. One of the other workers saw her. When we checked her, she did indeed have the money in her pocket. You see, Maria, this is a sure case."

I immediately began to cry. How could this be? I was just at home with my mother that morning. What was going to happen now? Where was I going to go? It seemed like a thousand thoughts were echoing through my head all at once.

Detective Nuevo gave me a tissue and said, "You are going to have to be strong about this. Your mother is very upset and she doesn't want to lose you."

Lose me? I thought. *Lose me where?* I sniffled and asked, "Is my mother going to be all right?"

Detective Gonzales replied, "That is not for us to decide. That is for the court to determine."

All at once, I felt as if I couldn't move. My legs felt numb and my stomach was doing flip flops. By this time, I was bawling uncontrollably.

Detective Gonzales said, "Don't cry, Maria. I'm sure she will be all right." He assured me that he wouldn't leave until I was calm and collected. *Calm and collected*, I thought.

How am I going to be calm and collected when my entire world is crumbling around me?

All at once I blurted out, "What is going to happen to my mother and me?" Detective Gonzales started in by saying, "Your mother will have to be charged and arraigned on grand larceny charges tomorrow. At that time, the court will determine if she will be set free, or if she will be held for trial, depending how she pleads. If she pleads guilty, she will have to come back for sentencing."

Everything was happening so fast, I could barely keep up. My thoughts were scattered. "Sentencing?" I repeated.

"Yes, this charge could be fairly serious and your mother could spend six months in jail," said Detective Nuevo." *Jail!* I thought. *How could things get worse?*

I began to feel light-headed and nauseous. I couldn't believe my mother, who had always taught me to be honest and hard-working, could end up in prison for stealing. I was angry and felt like punching the wall. I had never felt so frustrated and alone in my life. Even when things were so bad that we felt like we were not going to get another meal for days, I still thought there was hope. Now I felt things were hopeless.

I could not help but wonder why she had done this. How could she have been so destructive to our lives? I said to the detectives in a loud voice, "It's all my fault."

Detective Gonzales asked, "Why is that?"

I said, "If she didn't have to worry about me all the time, she wouldn't have done this."

Detective Nuevo responded, "It isn't your fault. You must never think that. A parent loves her children and would do almost anything for them. I'm sure Anita is a fine mother and the court will take that into consideration."

I shouted, "But if I wouldn't have—"

Detective Gonzales cut me off and said, "No, Maria. It is not your fault. You must never blame yourself."

By now my tears had slowed and my emotions had swung from frightened sorrow to sudden resentment. I was in a terrible predicament with no clear way out. I blurted out, "So what's going to happen to me?"

Detective Gonzales said, "That's a good question. It depends on a few things."

I asked with a sniffle, "What things?"

He said, "Well, if you have any immediate relatives in the area, I can release you to them. Then Child Services will get involved to make sure you are all right until we place you."

"What do you mean, place me?" I asked.

Detective Nuevo replied, "If Child Services sees that your relative is fit, then they will be given temporary custody of you. You'll live with them until further notice."

I asked, "But what if I don't have an immediate relative that will take me?"

He said, "Then you will be temporarily held at a Child Services home until we can find suitable accommodation for you."

I turned to the principal, with brimming eyes, and asked, "What?"

Detective Gonzales gently grabbed my hand and said, "If you don't have a relative, we have to find a responsible home for you. Until that time, you will have to live in a Child Services center in Monterrey. Once we find you a temporary home, we must wait until we find out what is going to happen to your mother. Then we will determine what your long-term living situation will be. At that time, we will evaluate your mother and determine if she is fit to retain custody of you."

I yelled, "My mother is a good mother and she is fit to take care of me! She always wants the best for me."

Detective Gonzales said, "We know Anita is a good mother because we did research on her this morning. She seems to be a very good, kind-hearted person. I'm sure she takes care of you the best she can. This is not for us to decide. It is for Child Services and the local court to determine what to do."

I shrugged my shoulders, sighed, and said, "Can I see her?"

Detective Gonzales said, "I'm sorry, but you can't. She is in a holding cell and you won't be able to see her until she is thoroughly evaluated."

I frowned and said, "Evaluated for what?"

He said, "To make sure she is safe. We have to make sure she is not harmful to herself or anyone else."

Detective Nuevo calmly asked, "Do you have any close relatives we could release you to?"

I sighed as slight tears were still running down my cheeks. I said, "Mama has a sister that lives in Juarez. I haven't seen her since I was two years old. I don't remember much about her, but her name is Linda Mendez."

He said, "Are you sure you don't have any closer relatives?"

I said, "No, but we have a friend named Antonio Soto, who lives in Mexico City. He just moved there a month ago."

Detective Gonzales said, "I'm sorry, Maria. It has to be a relative. We couldn't release you to a friend."

I said, "But Antonio is our closest friend and he knew my father!"

The detective said, "We can't."

I thought, *If Antonio was here he would make the police see that I could be released to him.* He would make sure everything would go back to normal. I thought that if he hadn't moved, this probably would not have happened.

Detective Nuevo said, "All right, Maria. We are going to try to locate your Aunt Linda. If we can find her, she can come and get you. You'll have to live with her for a while until things get sorted out. If not, we will have to find you a foster home. Foster homes can be very helpful with your problems. Most of the time these homes are with people that Child Services recommends. They are usually positive, uplifting, and sometimes fun."

All of a sudden I said, "I don't want a foster home. I want my mother."

Detective Gonzales said, "I'll tell you what, Maria. I'll follow your case and I'll do my best to help you in any way I can. I am the kind of person that will stick by what he says and will follow through."

Detective Gonzales paused for a moment and went on, "I'm going to ask a favor of you. I made a promise to you that I would help you in any way I can, but I need a promise from you. I need you to promise me to be strong and not cause any trouble. You see, if you cause trouble, it will not help your mother's case to get you back. She needs you to be strong so that she can get through this. In essence, she needs your help."

I thought for a moment, then nodded my head in agreement and told him that I would do my best to be strong.

He said, "We are going to call your Aunt Linda now. In the meantime, you might have to spend the night at Child Services. Now, Maria, remember your promise. Be faithful and strong for your mother's sake and I'll keep an eye on you."

Then he asked me to wait outside with the principal's secretary, Mrs. Mota. He said, "I have to discuss a few things with the principal."

I thought Detective Gonzales was a nice enough fellow, all things considered. I did believe he would watch over me, and I felt like I needed all the help I could get about now. So I figured I had better keep my part of the bargain.

As Mrs. Mota and I walked out of the room, Detective Gonzales said, "Maria, I know this is a great deal for you to handle at your age. Stay strong. Things have a way of working out."

Working out, I thought. *How could things work out?* I lived alone with my mother, who had just been arrested for larceny. We had been struggling terribly before this happened. How were we ever going to make things work now?

I didn't even know where I was going to spend the night, or where I would end up tomorrow. I kept thinking, *Work out?* I didn't know if I could see my mother soon, or if she was going to jail. I didn't know if Aunt Linda would come and help me. It had been so long since I had seen her. I thought maybe she wouldn't care. *Work out,* I thought, *He must be crazy.*

My tears had just about dried by now. As the door to Principal Ricardo's office shut, I swallowed the lump in my throat. Mrs. Mota asked if she could get me anything, but I said "no." I was just so distraught about everything. I was empty, lonesome and scared.

I could hear the detectives and the principal talking slightly through the old, worn wooden door. Mrs. Mota got distracted by a student in the hall outside the office and left her post. As she proceeded out into the hall, I left my chair and lurked outside Principal Ricardo's door. I heard Detective Gonzales saying, "It's a shame that a twelve-year-old was put in this position. Didn't anyone know that her mother was struggling so badly?"

Principal Ricardo said, "Half of the students in this school are in similar situations. It is just so hard to keep track of who needs help. And even if we had the resources, you know how it is. This is an impoverished area and it's very difficult to get help. As you well know, the government can be of little assistance in these matters."

Detective Nuevo said, "Her situation is a little different, though. With her father dying ten years ago, she should have been able to get help. Maybe she has had it a little worse than usual."

The next part brought a tear back to my eye. Detective Gonzales said, "Well, I hope it will work out, because you know how hard and strict the courts are around here. It looks like Maria will have to spend a couple of days at Child Services until we can find her foster care."

As another tear rolled down my cheek, I heard him continue, "Maria and I have an agreement. I'll keep my part of the bargain. From time to time I will check on her to make sure she is doing well. I just hope she keeps her end of the agreement and stays out of trouble." A slight feeling of relief came over me then.

Just then, Mrs. Mota came into the office and said, "Hey, Maria, no eavesdropping! Come over here and sit down." As I crept back to my chair, I couldn't help feel as if I had been abandoned.

Principal Ricardo came out of his office and told me, "You'll have to wait here for an hour or so with Mrs. Mota while we try to get in contact with your Aunt Linda."

I had puffy red eyes and my face was swollen from crying so hard. Mrs. Mota asked me again if she could do anything for me. I just shook my head. I had so many unanswered questions running through my mind. I was ready to just wake up from this bad dream that was now my life.

I was just a frightened twelve-year-old girl and didn't want any more instability in my life. So I closed my eyes, took a deep breath, and prayed that everything would go back to normal. I must have dozed off.

The next thing I knew, Principal Ricardo was standing there, saying, "Maria, we put a call out to your Aunt Linda and we haven't heard from her yet. If we don't hear from her in the next half an hour or so, you will have to go with Detective Gonzales and Detective Nuevo to Child Services. I really want the best for you. I hope everything works out."

I was able to muster a "thank you" that seemed to startle Principal Ricardo. Then he touched my hand and said, "You are a good student and a good person. Everything will be fine. I just know it will."

By this time, school had ended. My time was really getting short. I had a feeling I was going to have to leave soon with Detective Gonzales and Detective Nuevo. It just seemed hopeless that Aunt Linda was going to call. As I thought about my mother, a sadness came over me.

Approximately thirty minutes after school ended, Detective Gonzales came in and said, "We are going to have to go overnight to a Child Services home. It's called Santa

Maria's Home for Girls. Tomorrow we will try to find you a nice foster home for a day or two until we can contact your aunt. At that time, if your Aunt Linda will take temporary custody of you, you can live with her until we determine what will happen to your mother."

I blurted out, "But I don't want to go to a Child Services home."

Detective Gonzales said, "You must. It's a very pleasant place. You'll be with girls from all over the area who might be in similar situations as yourself. You'll get to eat three meals a day. You may even learn a few new things there. It's really not that bad."

He continued by saying, "You do remember our agreement, don't you?"

I nodded and said, "Yes."

He said, "Remember, Maria, you aren't going to make any trouble and I'll keep an eye on you."

I said, "Yes, I remember."

Detective Gonzales replied, "Then we must leave for Santa Maria's."

I had never been a troublemaker, so I didn't foresee any trouble brewing in my future. But the feelings of dejection and loneliness weighed heavily on my mind. I remember feeling very uncomfortable, thinking that I might never come back to this school again.

As we walked out of the school, Detective Gonzales said, "Principal Ricardo will gather everything that you might have left here and hold it for you."

I asked, "Can we stop at my house and get a few things, like my clothes?"

Detective Gonzales replied, "No, we can't. You see, Maria, we can't go in your house and take anything without your mother's permission, even if it is yours." Then he tried to change the subject by asking, "Have you ever been in a police car?"

I just said, "No."

I had never been in more than a few cars in my entire life and I thought it looked intriguing. We had never owned a car. I had rode in trucks many times on the farm, but nothing like this, and I had most certainly never been in a police car before. It was a black four-door with black tires and a black interior. I thought it was unusual that the car was entirely black inside and out.

Detective Gonzales said, "Hop right in the back."

As I jumped in, I couldn't help notice a rancid smell that lingered from the seats. It smelled like old rotten socks had been left in the back of the car. The smell reminded me of the many times I had done the laundry at my house.

Detective Nuevo said, "The back doors don't open from the inside. We also have this cage between the seats to prevent any criminals from escaping. Of course, you're not a criminal and your ride today is a friendly one. The Child Services home you're going to is on the other side of the next town, and it will take close to an hour to get there. I think you'll find it a friendly place."

I asked again, "Are you sure we can't stop at my house and pick up some clothes?"

Detective Nuevo said, "No, we can't."

I said, "It really smells bad back here."

Detective Gonzales snickered a little and said, "I wouldn't doubt that one bit. You see, Maria, some people that don't bathe often have been in those seats. We have had many criminals here. In fact, you are one of the better people we have ever had in this car." He apologized for the smell and said, "It will go away after a while, so just try to relax."

It was going to be a long ride. On the way to the home, we didn't talk much. I overheard the detectives talking about a case in which some people had broken into a store when the store was closed. They said they had a few leads, but it was going to be difficult to prove the case.

The conversation was really at a minimum. I tried closing my eyes, hoping that this nightmare would end. I kept wishing I would wake up in my own bed and that things would be normal again. That surely wasn't going to happen, but I was desperate.

Thoughts of my mother popped into my head. The hope that this was all a bad dream slowly dissipated. Reality began to set in as the car sped down the dry dirt road. I knew things were going to change drastically for me. I still couldn't figure out why my mother had done this to me. I was scared, but I remembered something Mama often said: without hope you have nothing.

— 7 —

I must have fallen asleep. The next thing I remember was Detective Gonzales's voice bringing me back to reality.

The ride was over and his voice was an abrupt reminder that we had arrived at my temporary home. As I looked up, my mouth dropped in amazement.

I mumbled, "Are you sure this is it?"

Detective Gonzales said, "Oh, yes. This is it. Why, were you expecting something else?"

I said, "Well, yes I was. I didn't expect it to be so big."

He said, "It has twenty-two rooms. I hope you'll be comfortable here."

I really didn't know what to say. I had never seen a building that size before, other than my school. It was a huge difference from my small house. Even so, I wished I was home and things were back to normal. But they weren't, so I had to try to cope with things the way they were.

As I got out of the detectives' car, I looked up at the building and noticed it was even larger than I thought. It had a main entrance with double wooden doors with no windows in them. The building was one story high and had brown wooden siding. There were no windows on the front of the building at all. The parking lot was paved with black-top, which the heat radiated from.

As I walked up the front walk, I heard Detective Gonzales say, "I hope they have the paperwork ready. I do want to go home tonight, sooner or later."

By this time it was nearly 5:00 and I was hungry. Detective Gonzales labored to pull the heavy wooden door open. When we entered, there was a woman sitting at a wooden desk near the front doors. She was a short, stocky woman in her middle to late thirties, with brown hair and brown eyes.

As we entered, she said, "May I help you?" Then she immediately recognized the detectives and said, "Well, good afternoon, gentlemen. Is this the young lady you called about?"

Detective Gonzales said, "Yes, it is."

She immediately stood up and said, "Hello, Maria, my name is Mrs. Hondo and I am pleased to meet you. I'm sure you'll like it here." When she said that, my heart pounded hard and my stomach began to churn again. I could not grasp the fact that I might be here at Santa Maria's for a long time.

I think Mrs. Hondo knew how nervous I was. She said, "I know how you must feel. It must be a shock to come here so suddenly. I want to let you know that we are all here to help you in any way we can. We want you to feel welcome here."

She quickly made a phone call, then said, "Mrs. Bautista will be helping you. She will be down in a few minutes." She turned to Detective Gonzales and said, "All right. I need one of you to sign the paperwork and you're done."

Detective Nuevo signed the paperwork like he had probably done so many times before. Detective Gonzales beckoned to me and said, "Maria, can I see you in private?" We went around the corner away from the desk. He looked directly at me and said, "Remember, Maria. We have a deal. I would hate to see things get worse for you. As long as you behave and stay out of trouble, you shouldn't have a problem. I'll check on you periodically."

I nodded as gracefully as I could, considering the circumstances, and said, "Deal." I thought at that moment, *Why would I make trouble? That would just make my hopeless situation even more hopeless.*

Both Detective Nuevo and Detective Gonzales were actually quite nice about the whole situation. I could not help feel that the detectives both felt a little pity for me, and I believed Detective Gonzales would keep an eye on me. Both detectives shook my hand and told me goodbye, and that they would see me soon.

By that time Mrs. Bautista was quickly approaching. She had a sort of strut to her walk as she came down the hall. She looked like she was almost in a hurry, as if she had a deadline to meet.

Mrs. Bautista was tall, thin, and looked like she was in her late twenties. She looked strict and professional with her hair pinned back. She wore a snug outfit, grey pants with a white blouse, that made her look like she was trying to impress someone.

She came right up to me and said, "Hello, Maria. I'm Mrs. Bautista. I'm pleased to meet you. I'll be helping you get acclimated to our facility."

I just nodded and asked, "Helping with what?"

She smiled and said, "I'll be helping you get settled in for the night, and helping with your case."

"My case?" I said.

"Everyone that comes here has what we call a case. We do our best to place our girls in foster homes until their situations at home are resolved. I'm here for you anytime if you need help."

Mrs. Bautista asked Mrs. Hondo if Detective Gonzales and Detective Nuevo were gone. Mrs. Hondo replied, "Yes."

Just then a thought popped into my head. Would I ever see the detectives again? They had been nice to me and I did like them. If I had met them under different circumstances, I would have been more receptive toward them. I hoped I would see them again so I could thank them. We had a deal, so I hoped they would keep their part of the bargain. I knew I would keep my part, because I needed all the help I could get.

Mrs. Bautista broke my train of thought when she said, "Let's go, Maria. I'm going to show you around our facility. The first place I'm going to take you is the kitchen." We walked down a long narrow hall that was painted white. Despite its blandness, the place looked clean and neat.

As we approached the end of the narrow hall and large wooden door, Mrs. Bautista said, "This is the main entrance to the facility. If you enter or leave, it will be through here. We have several other exits but we don't use them unless there is an emergency. Do you understand?"

I said, "Yes." Then she opened the door and behind it I saw a woman at a desk.

Mrs. Bautista said, "This is Mrs. Escobedo. She watches the doors so no one gets in or out that shouldn't. You see, Maria, we are responsible for you. We must know where you are at all times and that you are safe."

I asked her, "Are we allowed to come and go as we please?"

She said, "Oh no. You see, some of the girls here might be in much worse circumstances than you. If we let people come and go as they please, some of these girls would run away and we would have a mess on our hands. We would have to notify the police that they left, and if they got hurt, we could be held responsible."

She paused for a moment and went on, "We do have a break outside during the day. And we do have times when we go outside on the playground."

As we proceeded down yet another corridor toward the kitchen, she said, "We eat three times daily, at 8:00 a.m., 12:30 p.m., and 5:00 p.m. If you aren't in the dining room at those times, we will come find you and find out why. These are the only times we serve food. We have seventeen girls here right now and we must keep our schedule. The kitchen workers work hard, so we always comply with the schedule."

The kitchen looked like the one at my school, but smaller. Most of the work area was stainless steel with two large ovens, two refrigerators, and a huge area for cleaning the dishes. The dining room was painted all white. It had four large wooden eight-seat tables and one green plastic four-seat table in the middle of the room.

As I looked up, Mrs. Bautista was saying, "We all go in line and eat cafeteria style, similar to a school atmosphere. Now let's go see the school area."

The short walk to the classrooms took less than a minute. When we arrived, Mrs. Bautista explained, "There are two classrooms, one for the older girls and one for the younger ones. Because most girls are here for a very short time, school is attended by the children on an age basis only. Since you're twelve years old, you'll be in room number two with the older children. I don't expect you'll be here very long. I read your file, and I suspect you will be leaving us before you know it."

The classrooms were small, about fifteen feet square, with plastic chairs and wooden desks. The entire room was painted white, as were all the rooms in the entire facility. On the wall there was a small blackboard that looked like it hadn't been cleaned in a month.

There were three small windows that propped open on a slant along the far wall. The teacher's desk was on the side of the room with the filthy blackboard. Alone in the corner sat a coat rack that was old and rusted.

"I'll bet you aren't used to a classroom like this," Mrs. Bautista said.

"No, I'm not," I replied.

She proceeded down the hall until we arrived at a larger room she called the recreation room. "This room is everyone's favorite place to go after they are done with their school work or chores."

I exclaimed, "Chores!"

"Yes, chores," she said. "You see, it takes an enormous amount of time and effort to keep this facility running. We are on a very strict budget, so we must work together.

Everyone has a list of things they must do to help. You may be required to do dishes, laundry, cleaning, or anything else when needed. We treat you well, so we expect help in return."

I didn't say anything and continued to listen. She then said, "I'll show you where the bedrooms are and where your room is specifically. The bathroom and showers are at the end of the hall." We continued to walk as she continued talking. "Your room is number eleven, Maria. It's just down the hall."

All the bedrooms were lined up along one hall that stretched around the corner into another corridor. She said, "Here we are. This will be your room. How do you like it?"

I gave her a half-hearted smile and said, "It's all right."

The room was very small and was painted all white, just as I'd expected. There was a single bed pushed up against the bland white wall. In the corner was a nightstand with an old brown, beaten-up dresser next to it. There was a small green rug at the foot of the bed on the cement floor. There weren't any windows at all in the room, which surprised me. I thought, *At least I don't have to share a room.*

Mrs. Bautista said, "Remember, dear, you probably won't be here for long, so don't fret. This is a friendly place and all the workers try to do their best to be pleasant. I know you don't have any of your own clothes right now, so I'll see if we can round you up something to wear."

She continued by saying, "Let's see. You will need a toothbrush and a few other odds and ends. You'll get a chance to meet everyone later, before bed. In the meantime, I'll see if I can get you something to eat. You must be hungry after all you have been through."

Was I even hungry? I didn't know if the feeling in my stomach was pure hunger, pure nerves, or a little of both. The fact that Mrs. Bautista was so nice helped somewhat, but her kindness didn't take away from the pain, anger, anxiety, and resentment I felt. I felt abandoned and still didn't understand why my mother would do what she did.

I thought longingly of the beaten-up couch that I slept on at home while Mrs. Bautista was approached by another worker. She was a heavy-set woman, very short, with small feet. She had light brown hair and chubby cheeks. She looked like she was about twenty-six to thirty years old and had a slight wobble as she walked.

Mrs. Bautista said, "This is Miss Sanchez, one of our mentors. Her job is to make sure everyone gets along. She also is in charge of making sure everyone is where they are supposed to be. She does all the scheduling around here, as well as many other things."

Miss Sanchez looked at me without a smile and said, "Hello." Although everyone appeared to be nice thus far, she seemed to be somewhat annoyed by my presence. She said to Mrs. Bautista, "The kitchen is preparing a plate of food for Maria. She will be allowed to eat in the dining room alone. Everyone else is done with their schoolwork and chores, and will be in the recreation room for an hour or so before bed."

Mrs. Bautista just nodded and said, "Good job, Bonita." Then she turned to me and said, "Your clothes and some other things are on the way, so I suggest we go to the dining room and see what the kitchen whipped up for you."

Mrs. Bautista's positive demeanor really made me feel more at ease after what I had been through. I felt like maybe she was a person I could trust.

When we arrived at the dining room, there were two girls wiping down the tables and sweeping the floor. As I entered the room, they looked up. One of the girls whispered to the other, "That must be the new girl. I heard she was from Mexico City."

The other girl started in by saying, "She looks sort of—"

Mrs. Bautista said forcefully, "That will be enough. Keep your mouths closed and your hands moving and we will not have a problem." Mrs. Bautista looked at me and said, "Remember what I told you about having chores to do? These ladies have kitchen duty tonight."

The first girl said to Mrs. Bautista, "We're done now. Can we go to the recreation room?"

Mrs. Bautista replied, "If everything is done, you may leave. Miss Sanchez will be in later to inspect the kitchen. I expect it to be in perfect order."

This was a side of Mrs. Bautista I had not seen before. She was firm and had a strict tone to her voice. She turned to me and said, "Take a seat. I'll see if your dinner is ready."

As she walked into the kitchen, a tear started to roll down my cheek. I thought, *Why am I here? What did I do to deserve this? When am I going to see Mama again?*

Mrs. Bautista came back with three large pieces of ham, a baked potato, a large helping of peas, a small salad, and two small rolls.

She set the platter down on the table and said, "This should be enough food to fill up an army." Just then she noticed that I had been crying, and added, "Maria, I know this must be hard for you. I realize you are in a strange place away from home, but you have to be strong and try to get through this. I'm here to help you and I won't let you down as long as you follow the rules."

I immediately blurted out, "When can I see my mother?"

She said, "We will try to arrange for you to see her in a couple days. We have a procedure we have to follow and the court ultimately decides when you can see her. I have studied your case already and you are much better off than most of the girls here."

"Better off?" I asked. "How?"

She said, "Most of these girls are here for much worse reasons than you. Some were raped, some were abused, some were abandoned, and some were even involved in minor crimes. Don't worry, though. There are no real bad criminals here. Most of the girls are here because they have nowhere else to turn. Until we find foster homes for them, they are here like you.

"I know what happened with your mother. I suspect she did what she did because she was broke and probably was tired of doing without things. That doesn't make it right, but I can see just from being with you, for this short period of time, that your mother did a fine job raising you. I believe you are going to do well here."

Everyone kept saying things would be fine. Well, I was wondering how. I had been taken from my school. I found out my mother was in jail, and I was put in a Child Services home, all in one day. I thought, *What's next?*

Mrs. Bautista said, "Go ahead and eat, Maria."

I was still very hungry, but I didn't feel like eating much. Even though Mrs. Bautista's encouraging words helped, I still felt lost.

After my first bite, my appetite returned and I started gobbling down my food. I guess my body took over and realized how hungry I really was. I finished my entire meal in a very short time, to the amazement of Mrs. Bautista.

After I was done, Mrs. Bautista came back in and said, "You must have been really hungry. You ate that meal like it was the only food you had all week." Then she began questioning me about how often I ate. I felt she had a genuine concern for me. After we talked for a short while, she smiled and said, "We must go over some rules now. First, I must start by saying, I think you are a good person and I don't see any trouble in your future as long as you follow our rules.

"There is no leaving the building without permission, chores must be done on time, you must not use foul language, you must respect the staff, and you must respect the other girls at all times. Do you think you can follow these rules?"

I said, "Yes."

She smiled and said, "Good. I'm sure you'll be helpful to our staff and the other girls. Now let's go to the recreation room and meet everyone."

As we proceeded to the recreation room, my heart pounded. I thought that if the girls were anything like the two I saw in the dining room, this could be a disastrous place for me to stay.

As we entered, I couldn't believe my eyes. It was a huge room, about forty-five feet long by twenty feet wide. It had windows that looked over a playground. The walls were painted with bright colors and decorated with artwork by girls that stayed here. On one wall was a huge, hand-painted soccer ball with a net beside it.

The room's ceiling was about two feet higher than normal, with carpeting on the floor. As I stared across the room, I noticed a table with girls playing cards. On the other side of the room was an old ping-pong table with four girls playing feverishly. In the corner of the room, neatly stacked on shelves, were twenty or so board games that looked worn from years of use.

I turned to Mrs. Bautista and said, "I don't understand."

She said, "Well, Maria, many generous people donated most of the things in this room out of the goodness of their hearts. Everything you see was given by one person or another who just wanted to help. Even the paint was donated to us. We rely on many people for support. All of the girls need a place to go to have fun and forget about life for a while. This is it.

"The playground out back is small, but we have a few swings and a couple of old pieces of play equipment for the younger children. There is a small field area where we can organize a game of soccer, baseball, or some other activity. We are very fortunate to have so many people helping us.

"Loss of recreation room privileges is one of the first punishments we use if someone gets out of hand. We don't allow anyone to use this room if they don't follow the rules. This room is a privilege. It shouldn't be taken for granted."

I had never seen a ping-pong table before. I had heard of the game, though, and was very eager to learn. I was just about to ask if I could try to play when Mrs. Bautista announced, "Everyone, stop what you are doing and come over here. We have a new girl to introduce to you. Her name is Maria."

Everyone briefly stopped, looked up, and said, "Hello" in their own unconcerned ways. It wasn't the warmest welcome, but I guess it was to be expected.

Mrs. Bautista introduced the girls by name, seventeen in all. It seemed the only names I could remember were the two girls that had been in the dining room when I arrived, Dolores and Sofia. I had gotten off to an unpleasant start with them and I didn't want any trouble.

The next thing Mrs. Bautista did was to ask Miss Sanchez to come over. Then she said to me, "I have to go now and finish a few things in my office. Miss Sanchez is going to help you from here. If you need anything, or are having any problems, you can always come and see me. Miss Sanchez, or the other leader, Mrs. Santos, who works during the day, are really good at resolving day-to-day problems.

"We only have about twenty minutes left in the recreation room until we start getting ready for bed. Remember, lights go out at 8:30 sharp. You must have a shower before then and get ready for bed. All of your clothes should be in your room by now. It was nice meeting you, Maria, and I'll see you tomorrow."

Miss Sanchez beckoned to one of the girls, whom she introduced as Cristina. She said that Cristina would introduce me to everyone individually.

My first impression of Cristina was unimpressive. She was thirteen years old, and had short, scraggly brown hair, old faded jeans, and a brown shirt that was too large for her.

At first I thought, *This girl looks like she doesn't take care of herself.* Then I remembered where we were and eliminated that thought from my mind altogether.

When Cristina first approached me, I was a little apprehensive about speaking with her. Then when I saw she had a huge smile on her face, I felt better. She shook my hand and said, "Hello. Let's go meet everyone."

She started with the four girls playing ping-pong. She said, "Hey, everyone. This is Maria."

An older girl stopped the game and said, "All right. Remember, we're winning nine-three. I won't have anyone cheating me out of points."

Cristina introduced Cassandra to me first. Cassandra appeared very bossy and had a loud, unruly tone to her voice. Cassandra said in a forceful tone, "Okay, this is Angela, Hannah, and Gina. Now back to our game!" Immediately she served the ball as if my presence meant nothing to her.

Miss Sanchez said, "Cassandra, that was rude. Can't you even take a minute and welcome her?"

Cassandra said, "I'm not getting any younger, you know. Nine-three, let's go!"

Miss Sanchez said to me, "Don't mind her. She's always like that."

Then Cristina took me around and introduced me to eleven other girls. Most of them didn't show much interest in me or even acknowledge I was alive. Only two girls made me feel welcome besides Cristina: Micaela and Blanca.

Micaela was a ten-year-old girl with long, wavy brown hair, brown eyes, and a nice smile. She also had worn clothing and a friendly demeanor. She shook my hand and said, "It's good to see a new face." I replied with a "thank you" and a slight shrug. I could tell that Cristina and Micaela were friends already.

Blanca was an eleven-year-old girl, with curly, light brown hair, hazel eyes, and a small scar on her right cheek. She walked with a slight limp and seemed a little slow. When she greeted me, she hesitated and spoke with a slight mumble. At first she looked a little odd to me, but at this point I wasn't being picky. I felt like I had better make friends with whomever I could, just to fit in.

Cristina said, "Let's go get a game. I'll pick one out that all four of us can play." She brought over a game called Clue. She said, "In this game, you go from room to room on a game board trying to solve a mystery." I had never played that game before, but I told them I would try."

We were just getting it set up and Cristina was explaining the rules when Miss Sanchez said, "All right, girls. Time to get ready."

Cassandra blurted out, "Come on, Miss Sanchez. We're right in the middle of a game here."

Miss Sanchez stated with a firm voice, "No, Cassandra. You know the rules. At 7:30, it's time to get ready for bed."

Cassandra was a tall fourteen-year-old with a strong, tough look about her. I could tell she was a real hardnose by the sound of her loud voice and her body language. Miss Sanchez said, "Now, Cassandra, or one day with no recreation."

Cassandra slowly put the paddle down and began to stroll toward the door. Miss Sanchez said, "Cassandra, you are asking for trouble. We are going to have a little meeting with Mrs. Bautista tomorrow about your sassy attitude."

Cassandra turned around and said, "I didn't do anything." Then she left the room.

Miss Sanchez turned to me and said, "Well, Maria, this is when we go to our rooms, get our showers, and get ready for bed. Most of the girls read after they are all ready, but they must stay in their rooms until they fall asleep. I'll get a book for you so you have something to read tonight."

I said "thank you" and continued to my room.

When I entered my room, there sat a pair of faded jeans, a brown shirt, and some new undergarments. The clothes were similar to what some of the girls were wearing. Others wore clothes that they must have brought from home.

In the bathroom were six stalls with toilets in them. On the other side of the bathroom, there were six private stalled showers. Six girls at once were allowed eight minutes each to shower. I put off my shower for as long as I could. I was very nervous being in such a new environment.

All of a sudden, I heard Miss Sanchez say, "Your turn, Maria." I was so nervous entering that bathroom for the first time I could barely walk straight. I didn't know what to expect. As I entered I noticed that everything I needed was in the bathroom — soap, a towel, and a new toothbrush.

After my shower, Cristina came up to me and said, "Maria, why are you here?" I just froze and couldn't say a thing. Suddenly, I was all alone and frightened. I started to breathe extremely heavy. I felt like everything was spinning for a moment.

Cristina said, "It's all right. Just settle down. You're having a panic attack. I've seen it before with another girl here. She was worse, though. Just breathe deep and relax."

I took short deep breaths until the feeling passed. I had never felt anything like that before. It felt like my heart was going to explode. I hoped it would never occur again.

I don't remember the minute or two that passed after that. I just recall Miss Sanchez saying, "Hurry up. Your time is up." So I hurried right along by brushing my teeth and leaving the bathroom. As I was exiting, Cristina said, "It's all right if you don't want to talk about it. We can talk tomorrow. Good night."

As I entered my room, a ghastly feeling of loneliness that I just couldn't shake crept over me. I tried reading, but couldn't concentrate. Jumbled thoughts kept racing through my head. I kept thinking about Antonio, and how this never would have happened if he hadn't moved away. Out in the hall, I heard Miss Sanchez say, "Lights out."

I managed to find enough courage to kneel down and pray like I did every night. Mama taught me to thank God for everything we had. She also taught me to thank God for getting us through another day. But as I knelt down that night, I couldn't think of anything to be thankful for. I had been through so much that my mind was blank. A tear rolled off my cheek. It had been the worse day of my life. In one day I had I lost my home, my mother, and my school. I was even wearing clothes that weren't mine and were a size too big.

I managed to ask God to forgive my mother for her sins. I pleaded with God to reunite us tomorrow. I asked him for help to cope and survive in this new home. I also asked him to send someone to help my mother and myself. I even asked him, "Why did this happen to me?" It turned out to be one of the longest prayer sessions I ever had.

After my last prayer, I hopped into bed, ready for this long, overwhelming day to come to an end. I wished I could wake up tomorrow in my own bed. Tears continued to flow from my already puffy eyes. I laid there helplessly, trying to come up with some kind of explanation as to why this was happening to me. I cried myself to sleep that night. The last thing I remembered was that Detective Gonzales had said that he would keep an eye on me. I hoped he would be true to his word.

— 8 —

The next morning I woke to a strange voice, one that I had never heard before. "Come on, ladies, it's time to get up."

I opened my eyes and felt groggy from the night before. It was one of the worst nights sleep I'd ever had. I had rolled and tossed around so much of the night, I felt like I didn't even sleep at all.

A woman walked in and said, "I'm Mrs. Santos, the day shift mentor. Come on, Maria, let's go." She was about five feet, six inches tall and had long, dark hair. She had a sort of toughness about her, similar to what Mrs. Bautista had.

I managed to say, "Where is Miss Sanchez?"

She said, "I work the day shift and Miss Sanchez works at night. Breakfast is in twenty minutes, so get some clothes on and get ready. Today is your first day of school."

School, I thought, *wow! Everything is moving so fast again.*

As I started to get ready, I heard Cassandra in the hall say, "I'm getting the seat on the end, got that? And don't even think about getting that seat for lunch either."

I already knew that Cassandra was one person I needed to stay away from. I didn't want to have any type of confrontation with her at all. I could tell from the way she had talked to Miss Sanchez yesterday that she probably couldn't get along with anyone.

As I entered the dining room, there sat Cassandra in her chair right at the end of the table. I didn't recognize any of the workers that morning. Cristina approached me immediately. Believe it or not, I was happy to see her. I actually felt less isolated when she was there. I followed her to the table and sat next to her with Blanca and Micaela.

As we waited, Cristina asked again, "What are you here for?" I just looked down at the table. A thought rapidly entered my head that I shouldn't even be here. Just then Cristina said, "It's all right, Maria. I'll tell you why I'm here. My father left my mother about four years ago. My mother decided she was going to go into business for herself. Well, her business was illegal. She would take money from men and they would, you know, have their way with her. One day, a man wanted to have his way with me. He tried to kiss me, so I hit him over the head with a lamp. He ended up in the hospital.

"My mother got in trouble and I ended up here. I don't feel so bad, though. In a way it's better than being at home. I don't have to put up with all that crap anymore. Anyway, when my father finds out, he'll come and get me."

Just then Cassandra interrupted, "Oh, sure he will. You haven't seen him in four years, but all of a sudden he is magically going to show up on our doorstep and rescue you from all your troubles. Get a grip! If I have to hear that story one more time—"

Mrs. Santos quickly interceded by saying, "That will be enough, girls, and I mean it. Breakfast is ready and I won't have anymore of that."

Breakfast was a welcome sight for me. I was used to getting a small breakfast and rushing off to school. This was different in a pleasant way. We had cereal with milk, toast, and eggs. I had to admit that this was a much better breakfast than I was used to. Blanca said she thought breakfast was better than at home, too. Even so, I longed to be home with Mama in my own house getting ready for school. Blanca slurped her milk while Cristina said to me, "If you don't want to tell us, that's all right. It must have been really bad if you can't even talk about it."

Cristina went on, "Blanca is here because her dad likes to drink. And when her dad drinks, he likes to beat up Blanca's mother. When he's done with her, he goes on to Blanca."

Blanca timidly spoke up and said, "Cristina, don't."

Cristina said, "Look, we're all here for a reason. Most of the time it is not our own fault. We cannot change who we are or what has happened to us. It does not help by not talking about it."

Blanca said in a small voice, "If I want her to know, I'll tell her."

Cristina just rolled her eyes and said, "Fine. You tell her when you are ready."

I did not ask if the scar Blanca had on her cheek was from a beating she took. I knew from looking at her that she had to have been beaten up pretty severely in her short lifetime. I felt absolutely horrible for her.

I could not even imagine why her father would do such an evil thing. She appeared to be a nice enough person and I did not see her being a troublemaker at all. I had never been beaten in my life, and for a brief moment, I felt good about that.

Cristina continued with her probing questions by asking me, "Come on. Why are you here?"

I resented the fact that Cristina was so nosy. I had only known her for one day and here she was prying into my personal life. But I felt obligated to tell her something because she had told me all about herself and Blanca. I felt like I needed her as a friend to survive this ordeal. And anyway, I did not want to make a scene in any way.

I took a deep breath and said reluctantly, "My mother apparently tried stealing some money from a market that she worked at. We were happy and had a pretty good life before this happened. I really don't believe she did it. My mother is so honest."

Cristina said, "Maybe they made a mistake."

I said, "I'm not sure about anything right now. I have no relatives in this area so the detectives told me I had to come here."

Cristina laughed. I looked at her in a very belligerent way. She must have known I was furious, because before I could say anything she said, "Cool off."

She continued by saying, "Listen up. You are here because your mother tried to steal money because you guys were hungry. Trust me, you are a lot better off than most of the girls here. Do you realize most of the girls are here because of some kind of abuse, or even worse? Some of these girls have no chance of ever returning home. If they do, they will probably be abused again.

"Many of these girls have parents that are in jail long-term. Their only hope is to find a decent foster home, which almost never happens. The way I see it, you are better off than almost everyone in here."

Here I was feeling that my world was falling apart, while all the other girls' worlds were destroyed with no hope of any stability in the future. Some of them had no chance of ever having a normal family life again. Still, that did not make my situation any better. I felt alone and wanted this nightmare to end.

I said to Cristina, "I just want to see my mother."

She said, "That is not going to happen until she is sentenced."

"Sentenced?" I asked.

Cristina said, "When your mother is sentenced, she'll find out what she will have to do because of her crime."

I said, "What do you think will happen to her?"

Cristina said, "It depends on the judge and if he is tough or not."

Just then Mrs. Santos came over and said, "Come on, ladies. I don't want you to be late for school." We all returned to our rooms, brushed our teeth, and went to our classrooms.

When I entered my classroom, reality set in. I realized that I might never go back to my old school. I realized that I might never see any of my old friends again. I was distraught and felt very lonely. I knew I would just have to cope with things the way they were.

The classroom was partitioned off into two separate learning areas. I was put in with the older girls, who ranged in age from twelve to sixteen. There were nine of us in all. Each side of the classroom had a small blackboard with a chalk holder at the bottom. The teacher's desk was small, with only two drawers in it, and sat in the middle of the room. The area was a far cry from what I was used to, but with most of these girls only being here temporarily, it made sense not to have an elaborate room.

The teacher introduced herself to me as Mrs. Havea. She briefly went over some of the rules with me. They were standard rules that every school has, like no talking during class. The different age groups had different assignments for the day.

Mrs. Havea handed out assignments and had things under control when Cassandra blurted out, "I don't get it."

She came over as Cassandra continued, "This assignment is stupid."

Mrs. Havea said, "All right, Cassandra. If you are going to be disruptive, you'll be leaving again and seeing Mrs. Bautista later."

Cassandra said, "Yeah, I know. I just don't get it."

Mrs. Havea said, "Come up to my desk and I'll help you."

Cassandra got out of her chair slowly, walked up to the desk, and said, "Show me."

I knew from that moment on to avoid Cassandra as much as possible because she was trouble.

Lunch soon approached. With it came more questions from Cristina. I really wasn't ready to open up to anyone yet, and I tried avoiding the subject, but she kept on pestering me. The only information I was going to share with her was where I was from and that my father was a good man who had died when I was two years old.

In the meantime, I gathered as much information as I could on everyone so I could use it to my advantage. I specifically asked Cristina about Cassandra and what her story was. I wanted to know as much as I could about her, just in case she gave me a problem.

According to Cristina, Cassandra had been a trouble-maker from day one. Cristina claimed that Cassandra's father had left her mother for another woman when Cassandra was four years old. After that, her mother survived by dancing at clubs around the city. Then one day her mother got stabbed by another woman who thought she was taking her man away. Her mother went in the hospital and Cassandra ended up here.

Wow! I thought to myself, *That's quite a story.* I asked Cristina if it was true. She replied, "I think it's true, to the best of my knowledge."

What a hard time some of these girls have had, I thought. Suddenly, my life seemed to have been pretty good, until my mother had been taken to jail and I ended up here.

After lunch we all went back to school except two girls who stayed to clean up. Apparently the ones that stayed to clean would stay later at school to catch up.

The afternoon session went by rapidly. We were all assigned some form of homework. Mrs. Bautista, who just started her shift, was there right after school. She asked everyone to get their homework done and meet back in the dining room at 3:30 for chore assignments. Some of the girls grumbled a little, but I didn't hear any serious complaints.

We all went back to our rooms and completed our assignments. I was done just before 3:00, so I had a little more than half an hour left before we were all due in the dining room.

I spent the time praying and reading. I asked God for help with my mother. I asked him to send her back to me. I loved her and missed her very much. I just wanted things to be normal again. I missed working on the farm for extra money. I missed my school. I also missed seeing my friends and playing soccer with them.

I was starting to feel very lonely again, but I knew the best way to avoid this feeling was to stay busy. 3:30 came quickly and all of a sudden it was time to meet for work assignments. I was used to doing chores at home, so I felt the work wouldn't bother me.

It took a few minutes for everyone to gather, and for Miss Sanchez to begin. She started with, "Cassandra and Angela have laundry." I expected Cassandra to throw a fit but surprisingly, she didn't make a sound. She must have liked laundry detail or I am sure she would have made an issue of it. Then Miss Sanchez passed out all the other chores. She split us up into all the areas of the building such as the recreation room and the halls. She had given out the entire list when I realized that Cristina and I were left. Miss Sanchez then said, "Cristina and Maria, you have kitchen detail."

Several of the girls began to snicker. Apparently kitchen detail was one of the less desirable chores. I guess this was because the work was done while everyone else was in the recreation room enjoying themselves. It really didn't bother me that I had kitchen detail. I had done dishes at home for half of my life and felt very comfortable doing them.

Miss Sanchez said, "From 3:30 to 4:30 we will be going outside to play." I thought that had to be good news from the positive reaction of all the girls.

The large play area was about the size of a soccer field. There were three swings, a set of old battered monkey bars, an old rusted slide, and a grassy area for sports or physical activity. Right when we got outside, Miss Sanchez and Mrs. Bautista gathered us up and asked us if we wanted to play soccer.

All the girls but three raised their hands. Miss Sanchez split us up into teams and went over the rules, but I already knew them since soccer was my favorite sport. The game would last for twenty minutes.

The other team started with the kickoff. The game went on for about five minutes before the other team scored. We immediately came back and scored to tie the game. Then we scored and took the lead, and they countered. It was two to two. We each added a goal and the score was tied three to three.

Miss Sanchez then said, "Next goal wins." Cassandra was playing defense in her end, coming down the field with the ball, when she fumbled it. I rushed right in and stole it away from her.

As I advanced toward the net, it was just me and the goalkeeper moving toward each other. I looked up and saw an opening on the left side and kicked the ball. Sure enough, the ball rocketed right into the corner of the net. I scored the winning goal and the game was over.

Everyone was completely surprised, including myself. The fact I scored the winning goal didn't sink in until I heard all the girls on my team cheering and yelling. Cassandra came up to me and said with an angry tone in her voice, "Lucky shot, bubble brain. You couldn't do that again in a million years and you know it."

Miss Sanchez stepped in and said, "That will be enough. The game is over." All the girls went their own ways to do other things. Cristina, Blanca and I went to sit down and rest.

When it was time to go in, Cassandra came up behind me. She pushed me in the middle of my back with her elbow and said in a very belligerent tone, "No one makes a fool out of me. No one does that to me. Did you hear me? You better stay away from me, bubble brain."

At first I was startled and didn't know what to say. I had done nothing wrong. I'd just played a good game of soccer, but apparently, Cassandra didn't see it that way. She thought it was a personal attack on her and she probably wanted revenge. I hoped she would forget about it, but somehow I knew she wouldn't.

When Miss Sanchez finally called us in, we had about an hour to do our chores.

Cristina and I got to play in the recreation room while all the other girls had to do their chores, since we had kitchen detail. That meant we would have to do our work after dinner while the other girls all played. I was happy about that because it would give Cassandra time to cool off.

We were the only two girls in the recreation room and I was excited. I asked Cristina if she could teach me how to play ping-pong. I had never played before and I just wanted to try. She said, "Sure." The first few minutes I couldn't even hit the ball. All along she kept saying, "It takes a lot of practice."

Finally, after ten minutes, I got the hang of it. We spent the entire time laughing, hitting the ball back and forth, and practicing our shots. For the first time, since I had been abruptly taken from my school by those two detectives, I was having fun.

Cristina and I were becoming friends and it felt good. The hour went by so quickly. Then Miss Sanchez came in and said, "It is time for dinner."

Cristina told me that we were having meatloaf with carrots and peas. She said, "It isn't one of the better meals at Santa Maria's." I wasn't about to complain, because there were many times when my mother struggled to provide even two meals a day for us.

After Cristina and I got our food and sat down, Cassandra walked by, bumped my chair and said, "I hope you enjoy your dinner tonight, bubble brain." I couldn't help thinking that Cassandra would probably never forget what had happened at soccer. She had found a new person to pick on and it was me. I couldn't afford to get in any kind of trouble with the promise I made to Detective Gonzales. I knew I would be nervous every time she was around.

After everyone was done, Miss Sanchez came in and said, "All right, Maria and Cristina. It's time to do the kitchen, so let's get busy."

We got up, walked to the kitchen and awaited her instructions. She explained everything that needed to be done. We spent the next hour cleaning all the dishes and pots and pans, as well as the dining room.

We tried to get it done as quickly as we could so we could go to the recreation room. We wanted to play at least for a little while before bed. We finished with twenty minutes to spare. One thing about Santa Maria's, they sure kept us busy.

When we entered the recreation room, the first thing I heard was Cassandra's unpleasant, boisterous voice saying, "I won!" She was apparently beating everyone at ping-pong again and enjoying every minute of it.

Cassandra then asked in her loud and unruly voice, "Is there anyone else that wants to lose?" Then she saw that Cristina and I had entered the room and asked, "What about you, bubble brain?"

Miss Sanchez cut her off and said, "If I hear you call her that again you'll be punished. Her name is Maria and she is a person too."

Cassandra bellowed back, "Oh yeah, well, she thinks she is a soccer star after today. Let's see if she is a ping-pong star too."

At this point, I felt it was best if I didn't respond. I didn't want to make matters worse.

She continued by saying, "Come on. I've beaten everyone in this place. You're next. Well, can't you talk? What's wrong with you?"

I knew then I had to respond. "I've only played once and I'm not really good."

She said, "Come on. I'll make it quick."

I was fascinated with ping-pong and wanted to learn as fast as possible. I had really enjoyed playing it with Cristina earlier, but playing with Cassandra could be trouble and I knew it.

She told me to grab a paddle, so I did. I was extremely nervous. She said, "The first one to twenty-one wins." I nodded and managed to muster enough courage to say, "I really don't know the rules."

She went over a few of the rules and then said, "Come on, let's play." She did end up beating me twenty-one to one. I only got one point all game, and that was because she made a mistake and hit the ball off the table.

It was obvious she was very good at ping-pong and she made sure everyone else knew it. She rubbed it in by saying, "Maybe you're just not lucky in ping-pong like you are in soccer."

I felt like it was a good game. I got to learn more about ping-pong, while Cassandra got a chance to get revenge on me for stealing the ball from her in soccer and winning the game. I hoped that meant she wouldn't pick on me any-more, but only time would tell. I just wanted to fit in until my mother could take me home.

Right after the game, Miss Sanchez said, "It is time for us to go to our rooms and get ready for bed."

After I got ready for bed, I prayed as I did every night. This time it felt different from the night before. Last night, I had been angry when I was praying. I was still frightened about being in this unwelcome place, and I was still angry about what my mother had done, but I felt a little more relaxed.

I just couldn't believe my mother would do what she did. I prayed for help that night. I prayed for so many things that I forgot what I prayed about. I was desperate and all I had was prayer. The last thing I remember about my second day at Santa Maria's Home for Girls was Miss Sanchez saying, "Lights out."

— 9 —

Mrs. Santos' voice sounded foreign to me on Monday morning. As I heard her calling for us girls to get up, I lay in bed a moment in a daze, wondering where I was. I guessed it would take a while to set in that this was my temporary home.

The weekend had passed slowly, although they had kept us busy with chores and a few organized activities. I'd spent all my free time in my room alone, reading. I'd been happy to discover that they had a small library here.

I slowly got out of bed and got ready for my day. The laundry had been done yesterday and my clothes were all ready and waiting for me. As I dressed, a note fell from my shirt. It said, "Don't ever do that again, bubble brain, or else."

I had temporarily forgotten about Cassandra and her animosity toward me. I had hoped all would be forgotten.

But Cassandra had laundry detail and it figured she would do something to worry me.

I was so tired that morning that I was one of the last girls in the dining room for breakfast. We had oatmeal with fresh fruit. One good thing about Santa Maria's was that we had three meals a day. That was one thing I wasn't used to at home.

Cristina and I still had kitchen detail. I thought it would be much easier cleaning up after breakfast than dinner because the meal was much smaller. But we didn't have any extra time between clean up and school, so we really had to hurry.

When we walked in the classroom, a girl named Felicia was passing out assignments already. As I walked by Cassandra's desk, she put her foot out as if she was going to trip me. Luckily I saw it just in time. I stopped right in my tracks and stepped around her extended leg.

As I went by, she made an unfriendly face at me as if to say, "I'll get you sooner or later." I knew she was going to make things miserable for me from here on out. I had no choice but to do something about it, I just didn't know what.

As I sat there during my first assignment, I had trouble focusing on my work. I just couldn't stop thinking about what I was going to do about Cassandra. She surely didn't seem like the type that was going to ever forget about me stealing the ball from her. I knew she had revenge in mind. I was just going to have to out-smart her.

I began to think of all different ways to possibly resolve my problem with Cassandra. I thought that I should go to Mrs. Bautista and tell her about it. Then I thought I'd better not, because if I got labeled as a squealer, things could even get worse. All of the girls could be picking on me then, and I wouldn't have a friend in the whole place.

I didn't think confronting Cassandra would work because she loved confrontation and she would never back down. I thought about ignoring her. Then I thought that wouldn't work because she would just do progressively worse things to me until she got to me.

Reasoning with her wouldn't help either, because from what I had seen from her, it was her way or no way. After about an hour of careful thought, I decided the best way to handle my dilemma was to befriend her. As ridiculous as it sounded, I thought it would be the only way I was going to get her to stop picking on me.

Lunch was uneventful that day and I was glad. I knew I couldn't afford another incident with Cassandra. I was going to have to lie low and avoid her altogether, until later. I thought that at recess I could keep a low profile and pass the ball to her if we played on the same team in soccer. I felt like that would make her look good and might butter her up a little.

I got picked on the opposite team, so I decided it would be best if I sat out the game. I wasn't about to take a chance of having another problem with Cassandra, or my plan might never work. I was sure that if anything else happened between us, she would be infuriated and would never let up on me.

When Cassandra found out I was sitting out, the comments began. She said, "Hey, bubble brain, what's the matter? Are you afraid I'll score on you and win the game? Or are you just flat-out scared? Maybe you should go away and cry where no one can see you."

Little did she know that I could probably score on her again and win the game if I wanted to. I was a very good soccer player. She had no idea that I had been playing all my life. But I just ignored her and walked away.

That afternoon flew by. Before I knew it, it was homework time. After I did my assignment, I plotted out my plan. It would be a little more difficult because I had kitchen detail, but I had it all planned out.

That night after dinner, Cristina and I started our kitchen detail by cleaning pots and pans. The whole time we were doing our work, I didn't dare say a word to her about my plan to befriend Cassandra. I am sure Cristina would have thought I was crazy to even consider it.

I was very nervous that night. Cristina could tell something was bothering me. She stopped me a couple of times to ask if I was going to wash the same pots over and over because I was so deep in thought.

After we were done with our chores, I hustled down to the recreation room to put my plan into effect. My palms were sweaty and my heart was throbbing. Cassandra was beating Amel at ping-pong. Amel was a thirteen-year-old girl who played ping-pong with Cassandra almost every night. Cassandra was clamoring about how she was trouncing her seventeen to three.

I just stood and waited for the right moment. My stomach was a bit nauseated from the nervousness and anxiety that came over me. After the game was over, Cassandra asked, "Is there anyone else that wants to get beat?"

I mustered enough courage to walk up to her and say, "I'll play you."

She looked at me and said, "Come on, bubble brain. You only scored one point on me yesterday."

I responded by saying, "Cassandra, it's obvious that you are an excellent ping-pong player. I was wondering if you would teach me how to play. I realize I'll never be as good as you, but I would like to try."

Everyone that could hear us suddenly became silent and their mouths just dropped open. No one could believe I went up to her and said that.

Cassandra said, "All right. Maybe I could give you a few pointers. No one in this place is any good at this game anyways. I get tired of beating everyone twenty-one to nothing."

By now it was so quiet in that room, you could have heard an ant crawl across the floor. At that moment, I thought to myself, *Yes!* The first part of my plan was working.

Cassandra paused for a moment, then said loudly, "What are you all looking at! She'll never be able to beat me, so it won't hurt to teach her a few things. After all, there's no competition around here anyway."

At that point, everyone started talking again and resumed their activities. For the next twenty minutes, Cassandra and I went over everything she knew about ping-pong. She showed me the proper way to hold the paddle, the proper way to serve, and how to keep score properly.

I felt like my plan was working perfectly thus far. I knew that my problem with Cassandra wasn't over yet, but I felt like I'd made a good start. Only time would tell if the first part of my plan was successful. I hoped Cassandra would realize that I wasn't such a bad person after all.

Miss Sanchez came in and told us all to get ready for bed, right in the middle of our game. I thought it was strange when Cassandra simply put her paddle down, didn't say a word to me, and walked out of the room. Usually she would make a rude comment or say something. She just simply left as if I didn't even exist. I didn't know what to think, but one thing was certain. I had broken the barrier between us and it felt terrific.

I didn't look forward to going to bed that night. It seemed that every night after I prayed, I ended up crying continuously. I missed Mama and it hurt. I prayed for her and her safe return to me, then I cried myself to sleep as usual.

This time I didn't sleep through the night. I woke up several times, tossing and turning. In the morning when I woke up, I heard Mrs. Santos saying, "Wake up, girls." As before, my clothes were clean and waiting for me right on the dresser.

This time there was no note from Cassandra. I wondered if she was going to lay off me. I hoped things would change with us. When I entered the dining room, I walked right up to her and asked, "Can you help me again with ping-pong tonight?"

She actually smiled slightly and said, "Probably. After all, you need all the help you can get." I was surprised that I had enough courage to approach her since she humiliated me several times before.

At breakfast, I sat with Cristina in the corner of the room. I wasn't about to sit with Cassandra just yet. I didn't want to rush things.

After breakfast, Mrs. Bautista came into the classroom and asked to see Blanca out in the hall. As she limped out of the room, my curiosity was sparked. The next thing I knew, I heard Blanca yelling, "No. I won't go back again! I am not going!" She ran back into the room, went into the far corner, and yelled, "I'm not going!"

Just then, two workers and Mrs. Bautista entered the room. They took Blanca by the arms and escorted her out.

It was a frightening scene. She seemed so distraught. I felt so sorry for her, knowing she was going back home where her father had beaten her.

Our teacher, Mrs. Ramirez, said, "The court ruled that Blanca must return home. Her stay with us is over."

I felt sick to my stomach. I couldn't believe that Blanca was going back. I thought to myself that the courts must be crazy, and it made me afraid of what they might do to my mother.

Mrs. Bautista calmed down Blanca enough so that she could come back and say goodbye to everyone in the class-room. When she entered the room, the frightened look on her face was clearly noticeable. Her eyes were puffy and red from crying and she appeared to be extremely distraught. She couldn't even look at the class when she was saying goodbye.

The look of hopelessness on her face was one I will never forget. She looked like a frail, battered girl that was going to be thrown to the wolves. After we said our final goodbyes, a few of the girls started crying as she left the room. I wondered if they were crying because Blanca was leaving or because she was going back to a hopeless situation. Many of the girls at Santa Maria's didn't have much of a chance to ever have a normal life. For a moment, I thought that maybe my situation wasn't as bad as it could be.

I felt upset all morning long, which made the day go by extremely slowly. I was shaken and couldn't get that look on Blanca's face out of my mind. I was sure her going home was not going to be good for her.

Lunch couldn't come soon enough for all of us that day. When we were eating, I listened to some of the girls talk. One said, "Blanca will be back, you know. After her father hits her one more time, the court will take her away for good. I just hope he doesn't hurt her bad."

Another one said, "I can't believe the court allowed that idiot father of hers to have her back!"

Cassandra butted in and said, "If that was me, I would hit him right back as hard as I could, right where it counts the most! I would rip his eyeballs out if I had to!" I wondered if I really wanted to be her friend after that, but I figured it was far better than being her enemy.

I was lucky enough to get picked on her soccer team that day. I wanted to play on her team because I wanted to get on her good side. We played feverishly and the teams were evenly matched. The score was two to two when I got an idea. I thought that if I could feed Cassandra the ball by passing it to her, she might score and win the game for us. I figured then she might forget about the day I'd beaten her team.

Miss Sanchez said, "Two to two, next goal wins." This was my chance. I worked like never before to get control of the ball. Finally, I got the ball after an errant pass by the other team.

Just as I stole the ball I heard Miss Sanchez say, "Two minutes." That meant if someone didn't score in two minutes, the game would end in a tie.

I weaved in and out of players taking the ball down in their end. I slowed a bit to wait for my players to catch up and get in the play. There was Cassandra, standing on the other side of the net. I immediately faked to my right. I turned and passed the ball back to my left side, right where Cassandra was standing. She couldn't believe it. I could tell by the startled look on her face.

She had an open net with the ball coming right to her, and she kicked it. The ball went right off the goal post, bounced over toward the goalkeeper, hit off the back of her foot, and went in. The goal scored! We won! Cassandra scored the winning goal from a pass by me.

As we all put our hands up and cheered, Cassandra said, "I knew I was going to score. That was my plan." She looked at me in a pleasant way as if to show me acceptance. At that point, I believed our feud was officially over and I was relieved.

As we walked back into the classroom, I courageously turned to Cassandra and said, "Nice shot today. You were great."

She looked up at me and said, "Yes, it was. Just wait until tomorrow."

Then I said, " Cassandra, do you think you could teach me more about ping-pong tonight?"

She said, "I suppose," and she walked into the classroom and never said another word about it.

The rest of the afternoon was uneventful and boring. I could hardly wait for us to get out of class. I wanted to complete my homework and meet Cristina over at the recreation room as soon as possible. I couldn't wait to play ping-pong while everyone else did their chores. We played for the entire hour. I was getting better and even scored a few points that afternoon.

When we entered the dining room for dinner, Cassandra motioned for me to come over to her. She said, "You can sit at our table if you want." I could not believe it. She asked us to eat with her, so we did.

I was on Cassandra's good side! After dinner she said, "Maria, after you are done with clean up, we will play ping-pong. I'll be in the recreation room waiting."

I just said "All right" and began to clean the dining room. It appeared that my plan to befriend Cassandra had worked. I should have been excited but instead I just felt relieved.

That night I was in no hurry to get the kitchen done. Even though my plan had worked with Cassandra, I wasn't sure that I wanted to be around her all that much. She had a big mouth and that usually got people into trouble.

After we were done in the kitchen, we had about fifteen minutes left before bed. I scored six points on Cassandra that night. She beat me, but I was making progress.

That night before bed, I prayed even harder than before. I missed Mama and wanted to see her. It had been about five days since that dreadful day when I was taken from my home. All this time, I had heard nothing about her where-abouts. I was all prayed out and fell right to sleep that night.

The first thing I heard the next morning was Mrs. Santos waking me up by saying, "Mrs. Bautista needs to see you in the office." I jumped out of bed, got dressed, and hurried over to her office.

I was not nervous at all. In fact, I was excited. I thought that maybe I was going home and this would be my last day here. When I walked in, Detective Gonzales and Detective Nuevo were sitting next to each other on wooden chairs, along with Mrs. Bautista.

Detective Gonzales said, "Good morning." I replied with the same. He got right to the point. He said, "Maria, we finally got hold of your Aunt Linda. She should be here today or tomorrow to get you. She is going to take you to her house in Juarez. And you will be staying with her for a while."

I immediately asked, "What about my mother?"

Detective Gonzales said, "Your mother pled guilty to the theft charge and was sentenced to thirty days in jail. She has agreed to let your aunt take you until she gets out."

All of a sudden, I felt a little dizzy. Things were moving way too fast again. I said, "My mother pled guilty and is in jail? My Aunt Linda will be taking me to Juarez? What?"

Detective Gonzales said, "Look, Maria. Your mother could be out in just two weeks. They rarely leave people in jail for their full sentence. When she gets out, you can see her. In the meantime, your Aunt Linda has agreed to help you. I think things are going to work out for you."

I stopped to think for a moment, but I couldn't think of a single thing to say.

Detective Nuevo said, "Your aunt should be here either today or tomorrow. Things are looking up for you, Maria."

Mrs. Bautista said, "Maria, you can go have breakfast now. We will keep you informed if anything changes."

I got up reluctantly and crept into the dining room. I really wasn't sure what to think. I wasn't sure whether it was good or bad, because I did not know my Aunt Linda at all.

I thought of all the praying I had done over the last several days. I could not believe that there was yet another twist to my life that I did not expect. I felt let down, disappointed, even betrayed. I was going with my Aunt Linda, whom I didn't even know. I felt that nothing less than being home with my mother would make things better at this point.

I could barely touch my food that morning. Cristina could not help notice that something was bothering me. She asked me, "What's wrong? " I told her that my Aunt

Linda would be coming to pick me up soon. She appeared ecstatic and congratulated me immediately.

I gave her a funny look and said, "I'm not sure if it's a good thing or not. You see, my mother did not talk about her sister very much. I knew that they were close at one time, but they haven't talked but twice in the last two years. There has to be a reason."

When we entered the classroom, I felt distracted. I kept thinking about every possible scenario for my future. I wondered if my life would ever be normal again. I felt that same anxiety as a few days ago, when I had that panic attack that left me hyperventilating.

I took a deep breath and tried to calm myself down. I tried to focus on class to keep my mind off things. Mrs. Havea was passing out our first assignment when I started breathing hard again. I took two deep breaths and started to work on my assignment. I did the best I could that morning, but nothing seemed to help. I kept thinking, *Am I going to leave today, or will it be tomorrow?*

At lunch, Cassandra, Cristina, and a few of the other girls approached me and asked if I was leaving. I responded by saying, "I guess I am." They asked if I was going home. I just said, "No. I'm going to my aunt's house in Juarez." They seemed happy for me.

Cassandra spoke up and said, "I hope you like it there." She was actually being nice, something I had not seen from her before.

I said, "Thanks." I didn't want to talk anymore and just continued eating what little food I could get down.

Not fifteen minutes after lunch, my stomach began to feel nauseated again. I remembered to take deep breaths and control myself. Then Mrs. Bautista came in and said,

"Maria, your aunt will be here in a little while. You need to say good-bye to all the girls and get ready to go."

Mrs. Havea made the announcement that I was leaving and that everyone should wish me luck.

The girls all got up one by one and said goodbye to me. It was like I was going off to war or something. Cristina and Cassandra were the last two in line. After she said goodbye, Cassandra made the comment that she was sorry to see me go, and that she had one less person to beat at ping-pong. Cristina, on the other hand, was rather unhappy. I could tell by the pouty look on her face.

Cristina said, "You are going to have to give me your address so I can write to you. Then you'll know how things are going around here. You can let us know if you like it at your aunt's house and when your mother gets out of jail."

I nodded and said "All right" before I walked out the door.

It was just another twist in my never-ending nightmare of a life. Here I was about to leave with my aunt, whom I barely knew. I thought, *What happened to all those prayers? Why were they not answered? What did I do to deserve this?*

I wished I could have been more responsive to the girls when I left, but I was just so nervous and scared that I couldn't. When I entered Mrs. Bautista's office, Detective Gonzales and Detective Nuevo were waiting for me.

They explained that Aunt Linda had just arrived and was waiting for me. Detective Gonzales got up and said, "I'll be right back with her."

My heart pounded in anticipation. I wondered if I would even recognize Aunt Linda. I just knew she was a pretty decent person from what Mama had told me.

I felt nauseated again as Aunt Linda walked in the room. She was rather pretty and looked a little like Mama. She walked right up to me, gave me a hug, and said "Maria, I'm your Aunt Linda. You probably don't remember me, but I'm very glad to be able to help."

Tears began to roll down my cheeks, just like they had done every day since my mother was arrested. I felt scared and somewhat relieved, all at the same time.

She looked at me and said, "Don't worry, Maria. I'll take care of you." She gave me a firm, reassuring hug that calmed me a bit.

For the first time since the day Mama was arrested, I felt like things were finally going to stabilize. My feeling of helplessness had diminished. It was the first time since my mother was arrested that I felt like anyone really could provide me with a home.

Detective Gonzales said to Aunt Linda, "You will have to sign a couple of papers and you can be on your way." He then said to me, "Maria, do you remember our agreement? You said you wouldn't get in any trouble, and I told you I would keep an eye on you."

I said, "Yes, I remember."

He said, "It still applies. I'll keep in touch with you in Juarez. You must stay out of trouble. It will be much better for your mother if you behave."

I told him I would and thanked him for all he had done. I said goodbye to Mrs. Bautista and we were off.

As I walked through the big front doors on the way out, I thought that, as much as I had hated walking into Santa Maria's, and how scared I was, it really hadn't been that bad. At least I learned how to play ping-pong.

Aunt Linda held my hand as we walked to her old, brown, beaten-up car. She smiled at me and said, "This is not my car. I had to borrow it from a friend. My husband, your Uncle Carlos, needed the car for work. He is a carpenter and sometimes has to drive far to work, depending on where his job is. He makes a good salary and we own our own house."

She told me to sit up front with her so we could talk on the way home. I noticed that the seats were yellow cloth and had rips and tears all over them. The dashboard was old and faded from the sun and the front windshield was cracked. The car was old and dirty-looking, but it was more than my mother and I had had back home.

Aunt Linda said, "Maria, we have over a four-hour drive to Juarez. I just want to let you know, I got here as soon as I could. I had to borrow this car and get away for a day. I'm so glad you are here with me."

She continued, "I have several bags of your things in the trunk and in the back seat. Your neighbors, a boy named José and his mother, helped me pack some of your things."

I interrupted by saying, "How is José?"

She said, "He is doing well, but he misses you very much. He told me what good friends you two were. I gave him our address so he could write to you." I wondered if I would ever see José again.

Aunt Linda broke my train of thought by saying, " I guess someone broke into your house and took a few things. I think when people from your neighborhood found out that you were not coming back, they thought they could take what they wanted."

I immediately said, "What do you mean, not coming back?"

Aunt Linda said, "Don't worry. You are going to have a much better life now. It was very difficult to decide what to take without your mother there."

I asked, "My mother, where is she?"

Aunt Linda said, "She is in jail for two more weeks. After that, she will join us in Juarez."

I said, "What do you mean, join us in Juarez?"

She said, "Your mother was very upset about what she did. I know that she is a very devoted mother. I spoke with her about what happened. She wanted you to know that she was sorry for all you have been through. Your mother was very desperate. You two hadn't been having regular meals for some time. It hurt her so much to see you have to slave at that farm all summer and on weekends. She was hurt by the fact that she couldn't provide for you. She hated to see you go without. She felt so alone and desperate that she felt like she had to do something.

"You have to understand, Maria, when Antonio left, she had no one left to rely on. She felt all alone. She never told you this because she didn't want you to worry."

I just sat there and didn't utter a word.

She continued by saying, "You were going to lose your house soon. There was money owed on the house and back taxes were due. It was only a matter of time before you would be living on the street. Your mother knew this and was desperate."

Tears were rolling down my cheeks again. Aunt Linda was misty-eyed too. She had to pull over to the side of the road.

She hugged me and said, "Maria, you were going to lose your house, you hadn't eaten well in days, and your mother had tried everything. She even wrote me for help. All this was happening at the same time. She saw the money, was tempted, and took it. She wanted me to tell you not to be mad at her, and that she is very sorry about everything. The last thing that she wanted to happen was for you to be hurt in any way."

Aunt Linda paused for a moment, wiped her eyes, then said, "Maria, your mother loves you very much. She could not bear the thought of you living on the streets without a home. So she took a chance and got caught."

I looked at her through my tears and said, "It's all my fault."

Aunt Linda raised her voice and said abruptly, "Do not ever think that! Your mother said that you would try to blame yourself. So don't."

I nodded with tears in my eyes and said, "I miss her."

Aunt Linda said, "I know you do, Maria. So do I."

I was quite startled when she said that. She had not seen my mother since I could remember. I asked, "Well, why didn't you come visit us?"

She said, "Because of my husband, Carlos." She took a deep breath, sighed and added, "We will talk about it later."

That conversation we had on the side of that dusty old road was one of the most heartfelt, emotional conversations I ever had in my life. We both were crying. It was like Aunt Linda had a past that she was trying to shake. I felt she was hurting inside too.

After a few minutes, when we had stopped crying, she pulled back onto the road and began to drive again. She made me promise that, whatever happened, I would not be angry at my mother. I said I wouldn't as I wiped my eyes.

After I heard about how we were going to lose the house, I couldn't really be angry at Mama. She was just trying to do what she could so we could survive. She did teach me never to steal, though, so I was still very confused. I was sure she was sorry about what she did, and that she would explain the entire situation to me when she saw me.

For the first time since Mama was arrested, I felt pity for her instead of anger. All that anger and resentment turned to sorrow. I wished at that moment that I could have told her how sorry I was. I wished I could have told her how much I loved her. I missed her so much!

We drove for a while without speaking. Finally, Aunt Linda said, "You know, Maria, we have a pretty nice house. And we have a dog. His name is Sparky."

She must have seen the excitement in my eyes because I perked right up. I truly loved animals and couldn't wait to see her dog.

It got much easier to talk to her the farther we drove. I felt like she was a good person and she did truly care about my mother and I. When we were about an hour away from her house, she said, "Maria, I have something to talk to you about. Do you remember when I told you I had to talk to you about my husband?"

I responded with a "yes."

She said, "Carlos and I never had children, even though we have been married for seven years. We have tried, but God has never blessed us. I think we cannot have children. In the meantime, your Uncle Carlos has been a heavy drinker."

She continued as I nervously rubbed my fingers together, "He has a good job and never misses a day of work, but he just goes and drinks sometimes. We will stay away from him when he does."

After a pause she said, "I guess I could have left him, but he is a decent husband. He provides for me even though he lost interest in me a couple of years ago. It's not a perfect life, but it's not so bad. That's why I never visited you. He and your mother know each other from a long time ago, and they haven't been exactly friends."

She took a deep breath and said, "He didn't want me to come and get you, but for once I stood up to him. I told him I had to and that was final. He was furious! He will get over it, though. It's all right. He won't bother you because I won't let him. Anyway, your mother will be here in a couple of weeks and everything will be as normal as it can be."

Just when I thought things were finally going my way, Aunt Linda tells me that her husband is an alcoholic and an unstable beast. Or at least that's the way I envisioned him. It just appeared to be another thing for me to worry about. She smiled and said, "Give it a chance. It will be better than you think."

The closer and closer we got to her house, the more restless I became. I truly didn't know what to expect. The good thing was that she had a dog. I just kept filling my mind with thoughts of what her dog might look like. It pleased me temporarily while we continued to drive. I'd had never had a dog before. I couldn't wait to see him. I just kept thinking good thoughts about that dog over and over again.

We had a little less than an hour to go when I turned to Aunt Linda and said, "I'm tired."

She said, "Close your eyes and I'll wake you when we get there."

All the stress from the past week took its toll on me. So I closed my eyes and went to sleep.

The next thing I knew, Aunt Linda was telling me to wake up and that we would be home in five minutes. I slowly opened my eyes and looked out the window. It was a big city, which surprised me. I had never been to a big city before. In fact, I had never even been out of the rural area of northern Monterrey.

The sight of Juarez amazed me. The houses were lined up in rows that went on forever. I didn't know what to say at first. I managed to mutter, "I have never seen so many houses before."

Aunt Linda looked over at me and said, "Oh, you'll get used to it."

I was finally getting a brief taste of what the real world looked like. I had heard about cities like this from friends at school, but I had no idea that Juarez would be so different from home.

I asked, "Do you live in a subdivision like this?"

She said, "Yes. It's a small house, but I like it."

I suddenly found myself thinking that maybe living with Aunt Linda wouldn't be so bad after all.

When we pulled up, I was somewhat shell-shocked and didn't know what to say. Aunt Linda broke the silence by saying, "Remember, I'll handle your Uncle Carlos."

The house was large and well kept. I was used to living in a one bedroom, beaten-down shack with old, creaky wooden floors at the end of an unpaved street, so her house seemed like a mansion to me. I asked Aunt Linda if she was rich. She laughed and said, "Far from it. I know this seems great compared to what you're used to, but we are considered average around here."

I got out of the car, looked around, and said "Wow!" The house was a two bedroom ranch with brown wood paneling on the outside. The front yard was small, about twenty feet square, with a dirt walkway to the front door.

There was only one step on the small wooden porch, which meant the house was at ground level.

The back yard was large, about thirty-five feet long by twenty-five feet wide. It had a chicken wire fence around it, and the middle of the yard had a nice green patch of grass.

I asked, "Where is your dog?"

She smiled and said, "He is inside. Your Uncle Carlos is in the city repairing some stairs for a customer. I'm glad we don't live in the city because it is so crowded there."

She unlocked the door and the dog came running out. He was a cute little Border Collie, with spotted black fur and a touch of white on his belly. He didn't growl at all when he first saw me. He came running right up to me as if he knew me. I crouched down and said, "Hi, Sparky" in a kind voice, and immediately began to pet him.

I stood up, turned to Aunt Linda, and said, "I like him."

Aunt Linda said, "I knew you would."

I was happy for the first time in over a week, since Mama was arrested. I couldn't wait to play with Sparky. I knew we were going to become very good friends.

Aunt Linda said, "Come on. I'll show you around." So we walked in the front door and she began my tour of the house. The living room was about twelve feet square and was painted a light faded yellow. It had an old brown couch at one end of the room with two green chairs on the sides. It even had a television on a stand in the corner.

I asked, "Does the TV work?"

She said, "Yes, of course it does."

I had only watched TV a few times in my entire life, mostly in school during elections and other various governmental functions. I had never watched it in a house before.

I stood there in disbelief for a moment as she continued the tour.

She said, "Come over here, Maria. This is the kitchen."

The kitchen was good-sized. It had a dining room table with four chairs in one corner, and a full set of appliances. It had a stove, a refrigerator, an electric can opener, and a washer and dryer around the corner in the next room. I was flabbergasted. I had never seen a house before with all modern appliances in it.

She said, "Let's go see the bedrooms next."

Her bedroom was painted white with a double bed in it and a dresser off to the side, with a window over it. The bathroom was between the bedrooms, with the hall separating it from the living room.

When we got to the second bedroom she said, "This is where you and your mother will sleep." The room was painted yellow. It had a double bed, a dresser, and a small wall closet. The paint was slightly chipped in places and the light fixture was old and dusty. The window needed cleaning, but all in all, I thought it looked great.

She asked, "So, what do you think?"

I said, "It's terrific!" I just couldn't believe how nice everything looked compared to what we had back home. Once again I thought, *Maybe this won't be so bad after all.*

Sparky stood there wagging his tail as I took in everything about the house for a moment or two. I think he was excited because he liked me and he had a new friend.

I looked around the room and said, "Thank you, Aunt Linda."

She smiled and said, "Come on. Let's go get your things."

So we went outside to unload the car. We gathered all of my and Mama's things and put them in the spare bedroom.

I said to Aunt Linda, "I never had my own room before, except at Santa Maria's. I'm glad I'm here instead of there."

It seemed unreal that earlier that day I had been at Santa Maria's. Now here I was, in a nice house with my own room and a dog to play with. I thought to myself, *Boy, does life change quickly.*

Aunt Linda told me that Uncle Carlos would be home soon. She said, "He will not be happy. Just remember, I want you here no matter what happens."

Just then I heard the front door push open. When I looked up, there stood Uncle Carlos with his hands on his hips. He was about six feet tall, with brown hair and brown eyes. His complexion was medium in color, which was much lighter than most people that I knew. He wasn't fair-skinned, but he was much lighter than me. He had on dirty old jeans and a pair of old brown work boots that looked worn from long days of hard work. He had a slight scowl on his face.

With a timid voice Aunt Linda asked, "How was your day?"

After a moment, he finally said, "How do you think? I told you we can barely feed ourselves, let alone anyone else."

Aunt Linda said, "Please, Carlos, not in front of Maria."

Uncle Carlos said, "Take her back."

She said, "No. I won't."

He yelled, "We talked about this and we can't do it!"

She said, "Please Carlos. We have to! You know what this child has been through."

He stood there with a mean look on his face and said, "She'd better pull her own weight around here." Then he walked out and slammed the door behind him.

I couldn't move. I felt terrified. I couldn't say anything. Aunt Linda said, "Don't worry. He'll warm up to you. Besides, I'm here for you."

I turned around, ran to my room, and began to cry. She followed me. She hugged me and said, "Don't cry. I want you here. I would not have it any other way."

I said with a shaky voice, "Do you know why I'm crying?"

She said, "No, why?"

I said, "Because every time I think things are finally going my way, something happens and things get worse."

She said, "Just stay away from him and everything will be great."

Her words didn't comfort me much. I told her that I wanted to be alone. She said that if I needed her, she would be in the kitchen and then she left.

I felt uneasy most of the evening. When I went to bed at 9:00, Uncle Carlos wasn't home yet and I was glad. I wondered how anyone could be so mean. I didn't care to see him ever again. The way he felt about me meant trouble, and I was sure of one thing: I didn't need any more trouble.

I fell right asleep right after my prayers. The next thing I remember was a loud noise that woke me up. It was a thundering crash that sounded like the front door slamming. It was Uncle Carlos coming home for the night. It must have been 1:00 a.m. or later when he stumbled in.

He must have fallen, because I heard a loud bang. I was terrified as I managed to stumble out of bed to see what the ruckus was about. Just then, Aunt Linda saw me. She said,

"Go back to bed and shut your door." So I immediately jumped back in bed and pulled the covers over my head.

I heard Uncle Carlos slur a few words that sounded like, "I'm fine. Leave me alone."

Aunt Linda said, "Do you need help getting into bed?"

He yelled, "I don't need your help! Leave me alone."

I laid in my bed, clutching my blanket, terrified, as I anxiously wondered what he was going to do next. I heard a few more mumbled words and then it was silent.

I laid awake most of the rest of the night, worried that he was going to get up and do something vicious. I wondered why Uncle Carlos was so adamant about me not coming here. I couldn't think why he hated me so much. I didn't even know him.

I couldn't help thinking that maybe I had been better off at Santa Maria's. At least I'd made a few friends and things were well-organized there. It was a long, lonely night with scattered thoughts popping in and out of my head all night long. I was used to frightening, lonely nights lately, but this one felt almost life-threatening.

The next morning I woke up very tired, as if I hadn't even slept. Aunt Linda was in the kitchen doing some housework when I left my room. I yawned and said good morning. She asked, "Did you hear us last night?"

I said, "Yes, I did."

She looked sad and said, "He really is a good person. It just takes some time for him to warm up to people."

I asked, "Why does he hate me?"

She said, "Oh honey, he doesn't hate you. He is just a little put out. The fact that we don't have any children has hit him hard. We have tried, you know. We just haven't had any luck yet. That's not any of your concern, though. He will like you after he gets to know you. Just give him some time. Besides, you just let me worry about him."

My impression of Uncle Carlos was that he was a bitter, mean man who drank too much. I didn't like him at all, and he frightened me. I couldn't wait for Mama to come here so things could get back to normal. *Normal*, I thought, *How could things be normal if we were going to be living here?*

It looked like our old house was just a memory, and we would be stuck with my mean Uncle Carlos. At least he had already left for work. I thought the earlier he left, the better. Tomorrow was the weekend, but I hoped he would be working then too, so I wouldn't have to see him.

Aunt Linda said, "We'll have to get you enrolled in school."

When I didn't say anything, she continued, "You'll like it here. The schools are modern and have a basketball court, a soccer field, and even a few computers. I'm sure it's much different than your old school. You will like it a lot. You'll see."

It was hard to believe that I was actually looking forward to going to school. Normally, I liked school, but I was a bit apprehensive about meeting a new group of people. But anything was better than being around Uncle Carlos. I wanted to stay as far away from him as I could.

I helped Aunt Linda with the housework, then she and I went for an afternoon walk. I think she just wanted to show me around and for me to get familiar with my surroundings. The suburb in which we lived was a poor area, but it was far better than the place I lived before. I liked her house and her neighborhood a lot. I just couldn't get over the fact that Uncle Carlos was so bitter.

We walked about two miles and came to a park. It had a swing, a slide, an old, beaten-down, wooden teeter-totter, a basketball hoop, and an open field area for playing soccer. We spent the entire afternoon there, talking about everything that had happened to me. We talked about Mama and how much I missed her. That afternoon, I came to the conclusion that Aunt Linda was a very good person. I realized I was going to like her very much. It seemed like she truly cared about Mama and I.

Our long conversation came to an abrupt end when she said, "We have to get back. I have to cook dinner." I nodded my head and sighed as we began to walk back toward home.

I enjoyed that afternoon in the park with Aunt Linda. We never had anything that resembled a park like that back home. I wondered if the fact that she lived on the border of the United States had anything to do with having such a nice park in her neighborhood.

I had heard stories about the United States in school. I had heard that it was a great place to live, and that people could get real jobs and live in big houses there. It was a place everyone wanted to go and live. It had seemed so far away before. Now, it was just a few miles away. The border was so close it made me curious about what it was really like in the United States.

When we got home, Aunt Linda made dinner while I did some minor cleaning and laundry. I was good at that sort of thing and didn't mind at all. Aunt Linda told me she wanted to make Carlos something special for dinner. So she made him his favorite meal, tacos. She said, "I want him to warm up to the fact that you and Anita are going to be living with us.

"Carlos comes home at 5:00 almost every day, except when he stops at the local bar with his friends from work.

His day consists of eight hours of carpentry work and can be very physical at times. If he works later, he calls me to let me know he will be late." Since he didn't call that day, she expected him home promptly.

When Carlos got home that day, he walked right into the bedroom, changed his clothes, and sat down for dinner. After he got a plate of food, he said, "I will be eating out back."

Aunt Linda said, "Oh, come on, Carlos."

He stood up and said, "Oh come on, nothing. I want to eat outside alone."

Then he walked outside, into the back yard. Aunt Linda looked at me and said, "Don't worry. He does this from time to time. He must have had a bad day at work."

At dinner that night I was pretty quiet. I kept thinking of how I had befriended Cassandra. I thought maybe I could do the same with Uncle Carlos. After dinner I would try to talk to him.

The difference between Cassandra and Uncle Carlos was that I knew Cassandra was a temporary problem. Uncle Carlos was a permanent problem. It looked like I was going to live with him for a long time, whether I liked it or not. The other difference was that Uncle Carlos frightened me a bit, because he appeared to be so unstable. Cassandra was a bully, but I knew she would be easy to outsmart.

When Uncle Carlos was done eating, he came in, put his plate in the sink, and said, "I'm leaving."

Aunt Linda replied, " No. Not again tonight, Carlos."

He raised his voice, and said, "Get off my back," and he walked out the door.

Aunt Linda was left with a sad look on her face.

I said, "I'm sorry."

She replied, "Maria, it's not your fault. It has been like this a long time. He just shuts me out and keeps to himself. I'm so glad that you are here now. You can keep me company."

We spent the rest of the evening playing cards and watching TV. I thought it was absolutely terrific. Even though we only got two channels, I loved it.

Time went by rapidly that evening. Uncle Carlos still wasn't home when I went to sleep. I hoped he wouldn't bust in drunk again like last night. That night I prayed over and over again for my mother to come back to me. I prayed for Aunt Linda, because she seemed to be trying to help me as best as she could.

I didn't hear a sound that night and I slept straight through.

When I woke up the next morning, Uncle Carlos had gone to work already. I was extremely happy he was gone. Aunt Linda told me she had to go to work too. She explained how she worked two or three days a week at a local restaurant for extra money. She said, "You'll have to stay home alone for a few hours."

I said, "That will be fine." So I spent the rest of the day watching TV while she was at work.

That afternoon, Uncle Carlos came home first, around 3:00. I felt very uncomfortable knowing that he didn't want me there. He walked right in, changed his clothes, grabbed something from the kitchen without even saying a word to me, and went outside. I waited for Aunt Linda, who came home at 3:30. I thought this was the best time to work on my plan.

I went outside and sat down. Uncle Carlos was done eating and he was just sitting in his chair. I turned to him and said, "Uncle Carlos, why do you hate me?"

He looked up with a startled look on his face and said, "I don't hate you."

Now I had a startled look on my face. "Then why do you treat me the way you do?" I asked. He didn't say anything.

I said, "If it is the money, then I can get a part time job." I went on and told him about the farm and how I helped my mother out. I couldn't believe that he just sat and listened.

After I was done he said, "Maria, I don't hate you. I didn't want you to come here, this much is true. I have enough trouble keeping Linda and I from going broke. And with two more people, it makes it harder. I just don't know."

I pleaded with him and said, "Just give me a chance. I'll help. I can do all sorts of things. I will help, you'll see."

He smiled a little and went on just staring across the yard. Just then, Aunt Linda let Sparky out. I figured that I had worked on Uncle Carlos enough for one day, and that it was best to leave him alone now. So I spent most of the afternoon playing with Sparky that day.

I really liked Sparky. I felt like, without him, I would have gone crazy. He was so much fun. When he first went outside, he would kick all four of his paws up, two at a time, on the worn grass. Then he would run around the yard in a crazy way for thirty seconds or so, which would make me laugh. Then he would come up to me as if he wanted to play. I just loved playing with him.

Uncle Carlos, on the other hand, apparently had a dark side to him. I didn't know what it was, but he seemed withdrawn. I couldn't help feel that there was something inside him that was making him miserable. I just couldn't figure it out.

The next morning started just the same as the ones before. The only exception was that I felt a little more comfortable after talking to Uncle Carlos the day before. Aunt Linda told me that we would be going to church and then spending most of the day working around the house. She said, "We will have time to go to the park or something after everything is done."

Uncle Carlos left before we went to church. Aunt Linda told me that he never went to church with her anymore. She said, "It is a pleasure to have someone to go with."

After church, we went grocery shopping at a store in town. I was amazed at the town and how huge it was. I had never been in a real city like Juarez before. I had never even been more than forty miles from my house. When we entered the grocery store, my mouth dropped. I couldn't believe how big it was. I could not believe how many things there were to buy. I had never seen so much food in one place before. The aisles were packed from shelf to shelf. The whole time we were shopping, I just looked around in amazement, taking it all in.

It was nice that we had the car that day because we would be able to put all of the groceries in the back. Aunt Linda said that Uncle Carlos walked to the local bar most days and was never home. Sometimes he would hang out at his friend's automobile repair shop. They would have a few beers and play cards.

She said that Carlos going out was harmless and it would give us time to get things done. We caught up on all the laundry, cleaning, and errands that she couldn't get done during the week. The day went by quickly.

Again that night, Uncle Carlos ate dinner outside alone. I didn't have a chance to talk to him at all. At bedtime, I went through my normal ritual by praying long and hard about my mother. I must have been a bit over-whelmed, because after praying I fell right asleep.

I woke the next morning to find Uncle Carlos had already left again. Aunt Linda had to work, so I spent most of the day alone, watching TV and playing with Sparky.

The first thing we did Monday morning was go to the local school to get me enrolled.

The school was like none I had ever seen before. The exterior was wooden and painted bright yellow. The inside was huge, with a small indoor gymnasium that had a bas-ketball court and an area for spectators. The outside had a real playground with a slide and swings similar to the park by Aunt Linda's house.

The classrooms were cleaner than any I had ever seen before, and were about twice as large as the ones back home. The floors were a dull white with faded tile, but were still much better than what I was used to.

We went into the office and I met the principal, Mr. Casita. He was a short, bald man wearing an old brown suit that looked worn and dirty. He had old brown shoes and had a bit of a negative look about him. He turned to me and said, "Because your Aunt Linda called ahead, I have all your transcripts and you are ready to go."

After we were done filling out all of the paperwork, the principal told me that my first day would be tomorrow. I was excited and nervous at the same time. That seemed so soon!

Aunt Linda took me back home and told me that she had to go to work. She said, "I'll be back in about five

hours." She gave me specific instructions about what needed to be done around the house, then quickly left for work.

I spent most of the day doing chores and playing with
Sparky. I was becoming attached to that dog. He liked the
attention I gave him, and I liked giving it to him.

When Uncle Carlos came home it was the same thing.
He wanted to eat alone in the back yard, withdrawn from
us. That night, right before bed, the phone rang. It startled
me a little because it was so late, and also because we never
had a phone in our old house. It was Detective Gonzales
calling with good news: my mother was getting out of jail!
It had been two and a half weeks since she had been arrested. Apparently they were letting her out Friday. When I
overheard this, I jumped straight up in the air and shrieked
with joy.

After Aunt Linda hung up, she explained that Mama
would be here Friday for sure. I immediately asked her
about our old house. She just frowned and said, "Maria, you
won't be living there any more."

A tear came to my eye, which I forcefully tried to hold
back. Aunt Linda said, "Everything will be great here for
you. Just wait and see."

I said, "I hope so."

That night I thanked God again, as I always did before
bed. I prayed and lay in bed wide awake for an hour or so,
excited that I would see Mama again soon. I just couldn't
wait until Friday was here.

— 10 —

I slept through the night without getting up once, and I felt like I was getting acclimated to my surroundings.

The next thing I knew, Aunt Linda was saying, "Maria, you have to get up for school.

It seemed strange that I was living in yet another different place. I was getting ready to start school in a different classroom again, with new students that I didn't know. I was going to have to start all over again trying to make friends and fitting in.

My teacher's name was Mrs. Lica and she seemed really nice. It was a large class with twenty-six kids in it, including myself. Some of them looked a little scary. A few had earrings and talked tough, as if they were in a gang or something. I definitely wasn't used to this, but I thought that I'd better try to fit in as best I could.

When I was introduced to the other students, they didn't even give me a welcome. It was like they had been through this many times before.

After I got settled in, the day went by extremely quickly because I was so busy. I was still excited about my mother coming here, but I hardly had time to think about it because I had so much catching up to do with school work.

The first two days of school were uneventful. On the third day of school, I was approached by two boys and a girl who asked me if I wanted to go and smoke some marijuana with them. I said no. They were frightening-looking, so I got as far away from them as I could. It only took three days in my new school to realize that this school was a cold, hard place. There were so many tough kids that were way off track. They didn't care much about anything but getting high and causing trouble. They seemed hopeless.

Thank goodness Mama was coming home tomorrow. I felt things would be much better then. I couldn't wait. Thursday night went by slowly in anticipation of her arrival. When I woke up Friday I was so excited, I could hardly get ready for school. It seemed like it had been a year since I had seen Mama. I had so many questions to ask her.

At school that day, I made a friend named Nina. She seemed normal and didn't seem like a troublemaker at all. Many of the children at school were big troublemakers and I wanted to stay as far away from them as possible. Nina seemed different, though. I liked her. She had brown hair, brown eyes, and was thin as a rail. She had a nice smile and was very polite. I felt like she was someone I could be friends with.

Something strange also happened that day. A girl I didn't even know came up to me and asked me if I had any money. I said no. Then she pushed me and said, "Next time have some," and walked away. It made me feel very uneasy the rest of the day. I thought to myself, *Oh great, I have another bully to deal with now.* I didn't know how I was going to deal with her, but I figured I would find a way.

By the end of the day I was even more excited about Mama coming home. I was no longer angry with her. I just wanted to see her and didn't care about what had happened. When I got home from school, she wasn't there yet. As I waited impatiently, Aunt Linda told me she would arrive any time now.

Every minute seemed like it lasted an hour that afternoon. Then, finally, I heard a car, the same one that we drove up from Santa Maria's in. Aunt Linda said, "I paid a friend to go pick up your mother."

My heart pounded in anticipation as the door of the old car slowly opened, and I ran to the car as she stepped out. There she was! Mama was back! The moment I saw her, I jumped into her arms, almost knocking her down, and yelling, "Mama! I missed you!" Tears began to roll down my cheeks as they had done so many times in the previous weeks. I was so happy I couldn't think straight.

Mama thanked the driver and said, "I love you, Maria and I'm so sorry."

I looked up at her and said, "Mama, I love you too and I'm glad you're back."

She said, "Let's go in the house and talk."

I managed to whisper, "All right." I felt so elated I couldn't stop crying. All my bottled-up emotions from this whole ordeal came to a climax when I saw her. By this time, we were both crying. I could tell she was trying to hold back her tears, but she couldn't.

When we got in the house, we sat down on the couch and she began to tell me her story. She said, "First of all, Maria, I never meant to hurt you in any way. You know it has been very difficult for me since your father died. I did everything I could to keep us alive all these years. But things were as bad as they had ever been for us. We were going to lose the house. We had no money to pay the taxes. They were going to evict us.

"I tried everything to raise the money so we wouldn't get evicted. I wrote Antonio letters and there was no response. I wrote Linda and asked for help, but I didn't get a response either."

Linda said, "I wanted to help so much, but Carlos warned me not to."

Mama said, "It's all right, Linda. I know you would do just about anything for me if you could."

She turned back to me and said, "I hadn't made any money in the last week. We had not eaten a good meal in over a week."

I said, "I ate at school."

She said, "I know, but I just couldn't go on like that anymore. I was desperate and I knew the money was there at the market. I knew it was wrong, but I got tempted and tried to take it any way."

She paused for a moment and said, "I'm so sorry, Maria. I'm so sorry for all that I put you through."

Still in tears, I said, "It's all right, Mama. I'm just glad you're back."

We spent two hours that afternoon talking about so many things. She told me what had happened to her and about the jail. She told me that it was one of the worst places she had ever seen in her life, full of nasty people. She told me that many of the women were drug addicts who moaned and wept all night long. She said, "I'll never forget the awful sounds and sights of that Godforsaken place. I made a promise to myself that I would never go back."

She told me how the judge had been very lenient with her, because he could have given her six months in jail. She said, "The judge knew I had a daughter, so he went easy on me." She told me how all she did was think of me the entire time she was away, and told me that she was so, so sorry that she ever hurt me. It was a very emotional afternoon that I will never forget.

I told her all about the detectives and the promise I made with them. I also told her about Santa Maria's and how I became friends with Cassandra. I was just about to tell her about school and how difficult it was with the troubled kids there, when Uncle Carlos entered.

Thank goodness our tears were all but dried when he walked in. I couldn't imagine what he would have done if Mama and I were crying when he saw us.

I sat close to Mama when he first saw us. I didn't know what to expect. My mother greeted him with a pleasant, "Hi, Carlos." I found it peculiar that she greeted him that way.

He looked at her in a concerned way and said, "Hello, Anita. How are you?"

Mama said, "I guess I'm doing fine, considering what we have been through. Maria and I have struggled terribly since Miguel died."

He said in a firm voice, "I'll be honest with you. I didn't want you to come here. Linda and I have fought over this repeatedly."

Mama said, "Carlos, I know you and I have not seen eye to eye in the past. And I know you don't want us here. I'm sorry for the inconvenience. We will only stay as long as we have to."

He didn't say anything and just walked away. He went into his bedroom, changed his shirt, and left.

Mama looked at me and said, "Don't worry, Maria. We will only be here for a short time."

I asked, "Why does Uncle Carlos hate us?"

She said, "He doesn't hate you. He just doesn't like me. A long time ago, before you were born, your Uncle Carlos and I had several arguments. I told Aunt Linda not to marry him because he was a bum. Well, Carlos heard this and ever since that day he has been less than friendly. You see, I knew Carlos before Linda did and he just never forgave me. There is a little more to it, but for now let's leave it at that.

"We should be very thankful that Linda and Carlos are letting us stay here. Just be nice and be pleasant at all times and we won't have a problem."

I had so much going through my head that I found it hard to think straight. I told Mama I was going to go play with the dog in the yard. I needed some time to clear my head.

She said, "I understand, honey. I know you have been through a lot."

As I was outside in the yard that afternoon, I thought that even though Uncle Carlos was a mean and resentful man, I was going to try hard to make things work for us. I thought that we could be here for a very long time and I didn't want my mother to have any more trouble. We had both been through enough to last a lifetime. The main thing was that Mama and I were back together and that was all that really mattered to me.

After about an hour of deep thought while playing with Sparky, I felt much better. I felt at ease and hopeful for our future. I still didn't know how I was going to keep away from all those troublemakers at school, but I would just have to lie low and stay away from them as best as I could.

After I went in, Mama told me that we would have to share a bedroom. I said Aunt Linda had already told me that. Before bed, I thanked God for bringing home my mother. I cried when I prayed that night, just as I had so many nights before. But the tears were much different than those of the previous nights. These were tears of joy.

Mama and I sat up and talked about so many things that night. We talked about everything from our friend Antonio, to losing our house, to what my father had been like. Something Mama said before bed struck me as being peculiar: "This is our destiny and we shouldn't be bitter. We should be thankful." That statement made me wonder if she was glad we were here.

The next thing I remembered was waking up to the sound of my Uncle Carlos coming home drunk again. Mama just stayed there in bed with me while we listened.

He stumbled into his bedroom and fell on the floor. We heard Aunt Linda help him up while he mumbled, "Shut up. Leave me alone. I don't even want to look at you." After that I didn't hear another sound, but it was difficult going back to sleep.

When morning came, I was still happy that Mama was there. At breakfast she said, "Maria, I'm going to look for a job today. Work will be easier to find in a big city than at home."

I thought to myself, *Wow! Mama isn't even going to wait one day to look for work.* That's the way she was, though. She was always a hard worker.

Mama told me, "I'm on probation for six months and I have to report to a court officer once a week." I wasn't really surprised. I had heard that might happen from Cristina at Santa Maria's.

The fact that we lost our house didn't bother me as much anymore. I was getting used to living here and I surely liked Sparky. I was just pleased Mama was there and that we were safe. I still had not mentioned to her that school was filled with troublemakers. I wanted to find the right time to tell her that I was having a hard time staying away from all those bad people at school.

School was the same on Monday. I had never seen drugs before, but I had heard about them. I was sure that was what some of those kids were doing, huddled around together outside that day.

When I came home from school, Mama had great news: she got a job as a waitress. She said, "I will be working five days a week and sometimes it will be very long hours." Things were looking up for us, except we still had Uncle Carlos to contend with. I thought a couple of times that I would have to come up with a better plan to deal with him, like I had with Cassandra. I kept thinking he was different, though, because he was so mean and nasty.

When Uncle Carlos came home, Mama told him she'd gotten a job and could pay him rent for living there. He just said, "Sure, whatever." Then he got up, changed his clothes, and left for the night again. For some reason, my mother didn't fear him like I did. She talked to him as if she wasn't scared at all. Even Aunt Linda didn't stand up to him like Mama did. It was almost as if she had dealt with him before.

At bedtime, Uncle Carlos wasn't home yet. I wondered if he would come home drunk again. I told my mother how I had prayed for her every night and how thankful I was she was back.

Her first day on her new job would be tomorrow and we were both very excited. She said, "The diner where I'll be working is a nice place and is very clean. There are not very many restaurants that nice in Juarez. I'm very lucky that they hired me. One of the girls had just quit the day before and the manager wanted someone right away. It's funny how things work out sometimes.

"I don't know when I'll be home from work tomorrow. You will just have to help around the house. After school, do all your homework and then you can play with Sparky."

The next day was uneventful at school and Mama came home around 6:00. She was very jovial when she entered the house. She told me about how she did very well for her first day. She explained exactly how she placed the orders and how most of the people that worked there were very nice to her.

With a big smile on her face, she told me that she had earned a decent amount of money for her first day. She wouldn't tell me how much, but she told me the tips were great. She said, "I like this job very much. I never really liked working at the market back home, because it was too unsteady. It was just too hard to make enough money to buy what we needed. I'm going to be very frugal with our money and save every cent I can."

She was so happy that night, I couldn't bear to tell her about the troublemakers at school. I guess my problems would have to wait for another day. There was no way I was going to ruin the good mood she was in.

Meanwhile, Uncle Carlos was spending more time away from home than ever. It was as if he was unhappy when we did well. A couple weeks passed, and almost every night he came home drunk and stumbled into the house after we were in bed.

I finally had gotten up enough courage to talk to Mama about school. After all, it had been two weeks after she had gotten her job and I felt like it was time. Things had been going fairly well for us and I just couldn't keep hiding from all the troubled kids at school any more.

That evening I approached her after dinner and said, "Mama, some of the kids at school are troublemakers."

She asked, "What do you mean?"

I said, "Some of them sell drugs. A lot of them skip class and some get in fights, or worse."

She looked at me and said, "What do you mean, worse?"

I said, "Well, I heard one boy say, 'I'll shoot him,' referring to another student."

She said, "I'm sorry you have to put up with that. I didn't realize it was so bad there, but I need you to behave for a little longer. I have been talking to a person that brings illegal immigrants over the border. I have been thinking about going over the border to the United States."

I almost stopped breathing right there. I couldn't believe it. My mother was one of the most honest, God-fearing people imaginable. Before she got caught stealing the money at the market, she had never done anything dishonest in her life. Yet here she was talking about trying to go to the United States illegally. I was speechless.

She went on and said, "I already talked to Linda. She has some money saved that she can give us. You see, Maria, Linda and I were very close before you were born, but Carlos and I don't see eye to eye. I don't like the way he treats her. He has basically split us up. That's why he doesn't like me. And that's why he didn't want us to come here. I'm just not sure yet about the United States."

I couldn't say anything. I stood there dumbfounded. My dream was to live in the United States, but I wasn't sure if it was the right thing to do.

Mama said, "Honey, I love you so much. I just want the best for you."

After digesting everything, I said, "I'm scared."

She said, "It's not a sure thing yet, so don't worry about it. We might just stay here with your Uncle Carlos." I knew she was being sarcastic.

She went on, "Look, Maria. I love you and I wouldn't let anything happen to you. The worst thing that could happen is that the border patrol would catch us and send us back here. So don't worry. It might not even happen."

That night it was difficult to fall asleep. I couldn't stop wondering whether or not my mother was really serious about going to the United States illegally. I just didn't know what to think. All I knew was that I was frightened again, but it was a different type of feeling than when I was at Santa Maria's. It was like being frightened and excited at the same time.

I was definitely seeing a side of Mama that I had never seen before. She was one of the most determined people in the world when she got an idea in her head, but I was very surprised that she was even thinking about taking a risk like that.

It seemed like every time my life started getting stable, some other twist occurred that changed everything. I'd had so many sleepless nights lately that I figured one more wouldn't make a difference.

— 11 —

The next day was no different than any other day. When I woke up, Uncle Carlos had gone to work as usual. Mama said, "Keep quiet about what we talked about last night." She said that only Linda, herself, and me knew that we were considering going to the United States. She explained that it was just a thought, so I needed to keep it to myself.

Mama had to work again that day. She said, "Things are going well at work, so I'm going to see if I can pick up a few extra hours today."

I had to go to school, so I tried to get ready as quickly as possible. When I got to school, I wanted to remain unnoticed. The last thing I wanted to do was to get in trouble. I had a lot on my mind from our conversation last night.

I wanted to tell somebody that my mother and I were thinking about going over the border into the United

States, but I'd promised Mama I wouldn't. It was a hard secret to keep, but I had to because I didn't want to jeopardize our chances.

A few more days passed and everything stayed the same. Uncle Carlos was out drinking every night while my mother worked feverishly to save money from her job. I spoke to her a couple more times about the drugs and the people getting in trouble at school. She kept saying to me, "Hang in there, because things are going to change for us real soon." I wondered if she knew something I didn't, or if she was keeping something from me.

School was a challenge every day and it was becoming increasingly difficult to stay away from the troublemakers. One day, when I was outside, I saw a bad fight. A boy named Gilberto owed money to another boy, Eduardo. Eduardo punched Gilberto in the mouth and he fell down. When he was on the ground, Eduardo kept kicking him over and over again. It was horrible. No one would stop it.

I almost went to try and stop the fight, but I knew I couldn't. I knew someone would have kicked or hit me for sure. But I couldn't have gotten through the crowd anyway.

When it was all over, Gilberto was hurt badly. He was bleeding from the mouth and could barely walk away. I felt sorry for him. Eduardo ended up getting suspended for a week. Seeing Gilberto on the ground bleeding like that, with no one going to his rescue, was awful. It was a gruesome sight that will stick with me forever.

I knew there were a lot of mean people in the world. It just seemed like they were all at my school. That night I told Mama what had happened. She said, "Don't get involved in anything. Where we used to live was more of a country atmosphere where people respected and helped each other.

The city is a cruel place sometimes. Most people care more about money and status than they do about other people."

That night Uncle Carlos went out drinking as usual. Before bed I prayed again as I usually did. I felt a little uneasy and restless before I fell asleep but I didn't know why. I'd had many lousy days since the entire ordeal with my mother started. This one was not even close to being the worst I'd had. Nevertheless, I was restless and it took me quite a while to fall asleep.

The next thing I remember was the sound of Uncle Carlos stumbling through the door. This had happened many times before and was not unusual. But this time Mama and I woke up when we heard his voice bellowing from the other room.

Uncle Carlos fell, as he often did when he came in drunk. We heard Aunt Linda go to him to try to help him. As she did, we heard him say, "Leave me alone, you witch!"

She said, " Carlos please come to bed."

He yelled back, "Don't tell me what to do! You don't ever tell me what to do."

She said, "I was just trying to help."

Apparently he walked up to her and said, in one of the nastiest voices I have ever heard, "Well, don't." Then he pushed her. She fell and hit her arm on the table in the living room. The walls were thin and Mama and I could hear everything.

When Aunt Linda got up, Uncle Carlos hit her across the face. The next thing we heard was what sounded like another smack. It happened so quickly that she didn't have time to react. Then we heard crying from the living room.

Just then Mama got up and grabbed a belt. She rushed into the room, caught Uncle Carlos by surprise, and yelled, "You leave her alone or you'll have to deal with me again!"

Again? I thought. Mama must have had run-ins with him before.

Uncle Carlos mumbled, "She had it coming to her."

My mother responded by yelling, "I have told you not to ever lay a hand on her again. If you don't leave her alone I will call the police."

Uncle Carlos responded, "It doesn't matter. She will never amount to anything." Then he walked into his bedroom. He went and laid on the bed and passed out. All this time Aunt Linda sat on the living room floor crying.

It was one of the most frightening things I had ever heard in my life. I was terrified the entire time. I did nothing but lie in my bed, shaking. I didn't understand how a person could be so brutally mean. Now I understood why my mother had never visited her sister Linda before.

After I heard that things had calmed down, I came into the room where Aunt Linda was still crying. Right when Mama saw me, she hugged me and said, "I want you to go back to bed. I'll talk to you in the morning. Right now Linda needs me."

I thought that under the circumstances I should do exactly as Mama told me. I did leave my door cracked open just enough that I could hear what Aunt Linda and Mama were saying. I knew I would not get any more sleep that night anyway.

After a few minutes, Aunt Linda stopped crying, although she continued to whimper a little. My mother started by saying, "Oh Linda, I wish you would leave him."

Linda said, "I can't. He's a good man. He has just been drinking too much lately."

Mama said, "I know it is partially because we are here."

Aunt Linda cut her off and said, "No. You are my sister and I love you. I want you here. Besides, you have nowhere else to go. It's not your fault."

Mama said, "You'd better get some ice on your face. Are you sure you are all right?"

Linda said, "Yes."

I could hear my mother walk into the kitchen, get some ice, and give it to her. Mama said, "Keep that on your eye. It will help. Will you please leave him?"

Linda said, "No."

My mother said, "Linda, I'm afraid he will kill you one day! Please leave him."

"No," she replied again.

"Please," my mother pleaded.

Linda just said, "I won't."

Mama said, "I'll always help you if you need me. Carlos knows from years ago not to hurt you when I'm around. That's why he backed down. Are you sure you don't want to go?"

Linda said, in a sad voice, "No. I just can't do it."

Mama said, "I just can't understand why you won't leave him. I just don't see what you see in him. I guess I will never understand. But whatever happens, you are my sister and I love you. If you ever change your mind, I'll do whatever I can to help." She stood up and said, "By the way, you'll have a black eye tomorrow." Then she went and got some more ice.

All along, Uncle Carlos lay in bed, passed out and unaware of their conversation. After Mama gave Linda more ice, they talked a little more and then went to bed. I acted like I was sleeping when Mama walked in the room and didn't dare make a sound.

The next morning, Uncle Carlos was already gone for work when we woke up. It was hard to believe he could drink like that and get up for work the next morning like nothing ever happened.

Aunt Linda had a huge bruise on her arm and her eye was all puffed up. When Mama saw her all battered up, the first thing she said was, "He is such a jerk! I have a good mind to—"

Just then Aunt Linda cut her off and said, "Anita, don't say anything."

When I entered the room, I gave Aunt Linda a hug. An overwhelming feeling of pity came over me, but I couldn't think of anything to say.

I went to school that morning upset. My mother said, "I don't have to work today. I have many things I have to do." I thought it was somewhat peculiar that she didn't have to go to work, but I had enough on my mind with school that I didn't question it.

All day at school I kept remembering the night before. I couldn't believe Aunt Linda wouldn't leave Uncle Carlos, but I guess she didn't have anywhere to go. I felt sorry for her. She was in a situation that was never going to get any better.

After school, Mama and Aunt Linda were waiting for me. When I walked in, Mama said, "I have to talk to you."

I was a little nervous at first from the looks on their faces. They looked so serious, as if something horrible had happened.

Mama started by saying, "Maria, as you know I have always lived by God's laws and tried to do things that are right and just. Now I feel that it is best for us if we try to go over the border to the United States. I feel that God has a plan for us. I feel this is our destiny.

"A man I met has arranged for us to try to sneak over the border. He has set it up that we will meet someone in the United States who can get identification cards for us. He has also arranged for us to get a place to live. Linda has agreed to lend me some money that she has saved."

I interrupted by saying, "Aunt Linda, can't you come with us?"

She said, "No. My place is here with my husband."

I said, "But he hurt you so badly! Can't you please come with us?"

I looked at her in a pitiful way as she shook her head. Her eye was swollen shut and was beginning to turn a blue color from the healing process. Her arm was bruised too and looked like a piece of damaged fruit at the market.

She said, "I'll be all right. Carlos is a good man. He just drinks too much."

Mama asked, "Are you sure you want to stay, Linda? You could come with us."

Linda emphatically said, "No."

My mother said, "If you change your mind, we are leaving Thursday night."

She replied, "No, Anita. I'm positive. I must stay."

I thought to myself, *Why would she stay with him after all he did to her?* My thought was interrupted by Aunt Linda saying, "You two go and find what you are looking for in the United States. I'll do everything I can to help. You will be in my prayers every night. And I love you both."

I knew what I was looking for. I wanted a big house in the United States, with a good job for my mother and plenty to eat. It seemed like such a long shot for us. It seemed like the United States was so far away, even though the border itself was just a few miles away.

Mama said, "It's all set. We leave on Thursday." She turned to me and said, "Maria, I must go over a few things with you. The only things you can take are the clothes on your back. We can't take any personal items that don't fit on our person. Linda will mail our things to us as soon as we get settled.

"One thing you have to understand is that most people don't make it over on their first try. Immigration catches people every day trying to sneak over the border. They detain them and ship them right back to Mexico. But in the event we do get caught, there is nothing to be afraid of. We would just be coming right back here.

"You see, we really don't have much here to stay for. We lost our house. Your school is terrible, and we just are not happy here. We have to try something. Do you understand?"

I said, "Yes, I do. But I'm scared."

She said, "Don't worry. I'll be with you the entire time. I have it all worked out."

I nodded and said, "I'll be brave. I'll help you out as much as I can." She made me promise that I would not tell anyone we were leaving.

I was nervous, but I knew I had to be strong. I had to help Mama as much as I could. With just two days left before we were going to leave, I knew I had to get busy and pray. That night before I went to sleep, I prayed with all my heart and soul that we would make it to the United States. After I prayed, I felt much better. I almost felt confident that we would make it.

The next morning I was even more nervous, but I was also excited about the prospect of going to the United States. One more day and we would be border-jumping! I had heard many stories at school about people going to the United States.

All day long at school I couldn't concentrate on anything. I worried about getting caught. I worried about going to jail. Most of all, I worried about Mama and I being separated again. I just couldn't clear my head of all the negative thoughts I was experiencing.

That afternoon after school was spent organizing and going through our things. We had to decide what few items we would take and what would be left behind. It was a difficult and tedious process determining what was important enough for us to keep. It helped that we had only a limited amount of stuff since we lost our house.

I was very tired after such a long worrisome day. As I expected, I had trouble sleeping, knowing that tomorrow we would be risking everything we had. All the worrying I did, and all the risk that we were going to take was for only a slight chance to live in the United States.

My mother made me go to school on Thursday. She said, "I don't want to draw any attention to us." That day was worse than the one before. I couldn't focus on anything. The entire day was a huge blur.

After school, I organized all my things that I wanted mailed to us in the United States. When we were finished with all our preparations, Mama said, "Maria, you should take a nap around 6:00. There is a chance that we will be up all night."

Then she went over the plan and explained to me exactly what we were up against. She said, "We will be riding on a bus or in a truck with many other people that we don't know. All of us will be dropped off just over the border. We will probably have to walk all night." She explained that it was much safer to travel at night so the border patrols couldn't find us as easily.

She said, "When we get to the city the next day, we will have to find our contact. After we find him, he will set us up with a place to live. Then I will find a job."

The plan seemed so risky and dangerous. It seemed like an impossible task, but I felt like we had no other choice. We couldn't go back to where we had lived before, because we didn't have a place to stay, or a job, or anything. We couldn't stay here because my Uncle Carlos was abusive and my school was full of delinquents. I knew we had to go through with it. I knew it would be our destiny.

I knew that I had to be brave and not disappoint my mother. I tried to act as if I was confident and unconcerned. The truth was that I felt absolutely terrified. My stomach was in knots and my throat felt like it was swollen shut. I didn't know how I would actually be able to cope with the anxiety once we were at the border.

I tried to take a nap, but of course I couldn't sleep at all. I was so nervous, I felt like I might never sleep again. I felt like a lump of rubber as I lay there in my bed. I just couldn't stop thinking about all of the things that could go wrong. I kept thinking about getting separated from my mother again, and how I missed my old home. I thought about Antonio and how he used to help us if we were ever in trouble. I prayed for help that afternoon over and over again. I knew we needed it.

The next five hours, between 6:00 and 11:00, seemed to go by in slow motion. I would never forget the anxiety I felt that night, as long as I lived. It was like I was a lamb being led to slaughter.

The next thing I knew, Mama came into our room shortly before 11:00 and said, "Come on, Maria. It's time to go."

I jumped up and said, "I'm ready."

We started to gather the few things we were going to take with us. She reminded me that we could only take what would fit in our pockets. We took some food, water, a spare outfit, and a few other sentimental items such as some pictures of my father and myself when I was little. Of course, we had all the money that Aunt Linda lent to us, as well as the money that Mama had managed to save while we were here.

When we said our final goodbyes, Aunt Linda, Mama and I were all in tears. My mother thanked Aunt Linda for everything she did for us. After a long hug, we were off. As we left, I couldn't help wonder if we would ever see Aunt Linda again.

We walked about fifteen blocks to the meeting place and just waited. A man was supposed to pick us up there. My mother called this man Mr. Cortez, but she explained that it wasn't his real name. She said, "He told me that he didn't want anyone to know who he was."

We had waited about twenty minutes when a black, beaten-up pickup truck approached. It had mud all over the outside as if it drove through puddles all day long. When the driver got out, I noticed he was short, had black hair, and walked with a slight limp. The first thing he said was "Are you Anita?"

My mother said, "Yes."

The man told us to get in the back, so we both eagerly climbed in. The truck made three more stops and picked up four more people along the way. After our last stop, the man drove us out of the city to an open farm area where there were more people waiting, about thirty in all.

At the farm there was a man directing people where to go. He told everyone to get in line, so we did. One by one, he collected money from every one of us. Then we were informed that we must be very quiet through the entire excursion, and if we happened to get pulled over by the border patrol, we must not say a single word. After that, we all got on the truck as best as we could. We sat elbow-to-elbow with everyone else.

The truck was an old delivery truck, open in the back, with old, dirty canvas over the top to prevent anyone from seeing in. The body odor in the back of that truck was foul and rancid. It was horribly noticeable from the moment we got in. It reminded me of old dirty socks that had not been washed in weeks, and some of the people smelled like they had not bathed in years.

There were six other kids aboard, including a girl that must have been no more than four years old. As the truck began to move, I knew it was going to be a difficult ride. The roads in the country were not well kept; they had ruts and potholes everywhere. The truck was obviously old and worn-out from many years of use on the old bumpy roads along the border.

About two minutes into the ride, I started to feel nauseated. I began to hyperventilate. I remembered what had happened at Santa Maria's and how I'd learned to control myself when I started to go into a panic attack. I began to breathe slowly and I tried to calm myself down. It was no time for me to draw attention to myself, so I tried to think of other things. I tried to think about our friend Antonio, and how I used to play soccer with José back home. I tried to think about anything to keep my mind off of our dangerous endeavor.

Half an hour into the ride, there hadn't been one word spoken on the truck. I thought that maybe everyone was terrified like me. Or maybe they were just following the strict instructions that were given to us before we left.

As we were driving through the darkness on the dusty road, we suddenly heard a voice over a loudspeaker saying, "Pull the truck over." It was the Mexican border patrol. I was so frightened when I saw them, I almost threw up right in my lap.

When the truck finally pulled over, I was quivering. The officers approached the back of the vehicle and made us all get out. They started to ask us all sorts of questions, but they asked them so quickly, we couldn't possibly answer. Not one person on the truck had enough courage to say one thing. We were all terrified.

Finally one officer yelled, "Are you people listening?" Just then, another officer told us to wait right there. They all walked about twenty feet away and began to talk. They called the driver over to them and said a few words to him. After that he returned to the truck.

I was so petrified I couldn't move. My legs were shaking as my mother held me in her arms. I overheard the officers say to the driver, "You'd better get out of here and away from the border as fast as you can, or we will throw you in jail. We will lock you up and forget you ever existed." Then one of the officers yelled, "Now get out of here!"

After that we were instructed by the driver to get back on the truck, so we did. He turned the truck around and started driving in the opposite direction, back to the old farm where we'd started our trip.

The ride back was extremely depressing. Here we were with high hopes of making a better life in the United States and our dreams were crushed in a single moment. All the way back I kept saying to myself, "Thank you, God, for keeping my mother and I together."

When we got back to the farm and got off the truck, the driver told us that this was a normal occurrence. He said, "Sometimes it takes three or four trips before you actually get over the border. Everyone get in the barn and get some sleep. We will try again before morning."

By this time it was almost 1:00 a.m. and I was exhausted. The ordeal with the Mexican border patrol had frightened me beyond belief, and I was so tired I didn't really want to try again.

As we approached the barn, I noticed that it looked very old and had never been painted. It smelled of musty old animals from years past. But it was quite large enough to accommodate all thirty of us for a short period of time.

Even though the barn was dilapidated, Mama and I were happy to find a place in the corner and lay down on the dirt floor. The night so far had been a disaster. I just wanted to lie down next to Mama and feel safe again.

We slept for about two hours before we were awakened by the driver saying, "Everyone get up. We're going to try again." Right after the truck was fully loaded, I thought to myself that the reason no one gave up was because it cost so much to get taken to the border. And obviously there were no refunds.

As the truck pulled away from the farm, I started to feel nauseated again. I think Mama knew how I was feeling because she grabbed my hand and held it tight.

About fifteen minutes into the ride, the truck abruptly pulled off the main road. The ride became even more bumpy as the truck rattled along an off-road path. This continued for a little while longer, then all of a sudden the truck abruptly stopped and the driver got out and yelled, "Everyone get out!" He pointed over a ridge and said, "That is the United States! Now go!" The thirty people on the truck scattered with such fury it reminded me of wild animals being hunted. Soon we could no longer see any of them.

My mother and I knew we had a long journey ahead of us, so we immediately got moving. She told me that we had to get to El Paso as soon as we could if we wanted to have a chance of staying in the United States. She estimated that we had about thirty-two miles to travel on foot.

She said, "It's going to be a difficult trip," as we began walking toward the ridge. "But don't get discouraged, because anything in life that you want is worth working for."

It was extremely dark as we began walking, but the night sky gave us a little inspiration with its bright, shining stars. We could barely see off in the distance because of the ridge just ahead.

As we began walking due east toward El Paso, Mama reminded me that we had to be as quiet as possible along the way. I thought to myself, *You don't have to worry about me! I'm so terrified, I couldn't say a word if I wanted to.*

It was strange when we got over the ridge, like a totally different world. We could see the city lights of El Paso way off in the distance, but it was so dark we couldn't see twenty feet in front of us.

A moment after I saw the city lights of El Paso, I felt invigorated and motivated. I felt like we were looking at our destiny and we must make it at all costs. All the frustration I had experienced over the last six weeks had suddenly turned to jubilation. I was excited. I was determined. I couldn't wait to get there.

As we continued toward the far-off lights, Mama said, "The next six hours are crucial for us. If we can make it that long without being seen, we have an excellent chance of making it to El Paso."

As we walked, I thought of all the things that had happened to me over the last few weeks. I thought about losing our house. I thought about Santa Maria's and all the people I met there. I thought about the troublemakers at my school in Juarez. I thought about how glad I was to be back with my mother. And I thought about Aunt Linda and how she got beaten up by Uncle Carlos. I still thought she should have come with us.

We walked for three hours, until the sun began to rise. Mama said, "We will only be able to travel at night. Most people get caught because they travel during the day when the border patrol can see them." So we found some rocks that would give us partial cover from the hot desert sun, and we hid behind them from the border patrol, which would be out in full force soon.

Mama said, "The hardest part for us will be waiting here behind these rocks all day, but we must not give in. We must stay here or we will surely get caught. Most of the people that came with us will be caught by 5:00 today. They get so excited that they take chances. There are twice as many patrols during the day, so we will just wait here. We are not going to take any unnecessary risks."

We talked for a minute or two about how much better life could be for us in the United States. We talked about Mama having a real job that paid well, and owning a nice house with a clean yard with flowers in it. Then Mama said, "We must get some sleep because we will be traveling at night again."

It was early morning and I was exhausted from being up all night. So we curled up near the rocks for shade and laid down. Mama reminded me that we had to be very quiet because sound travels far in the desert, and repeated that we had to remain unseen. So we fell asleep right there on the ground, with dreams of our new life ahead of us.

— 12 —

We were awakened a few hours later to the sound of an engine off in the distance. When I woke up, I didn't remember where we were at first. Then it suddenly came to me. We were in the desert on the border of Mexico and the United States, trying to sneak across.

The engine sounded like it was about a half mile away and cruising closer by the second. As I looked up, Mama whispered, "Stay down and don't move. It's the border patrol."

My heart started to pound like a bass drum. We huddled together motionless behind our rocks. Even after we heard the sound of the patrol slowly fade off in the distance, we didn't look up. We just stayed motionless in that little bit of shade.

Finally, when it was safe to move, Mama said, "The border patrol rides around all day with binoculars, looking for any type of movement, so we must stay as still as we can. They even use helicopters during the day. That's why we must only travel at night."

I nodded and said, "Mama, I'm hungry." I almost never told my mother I was hungry. Usually, I just wouldn't say anything, because I knew how hard it was for her to get food back home. This time was different though, because I was famished. It was early afternoon and I had not eaten since dinner the night before.

Mama had a small bag with her. In it she had five apples, a jar of peanut butter, some bread, a box of crackers, a small baggie of carrots, and two jugs of water. We ate that afternoon behind the cover of those rocks out in the middle of nowhere. It felt good to get something in my stomach after that long night.

The temperature rose to about 95 degrees that day in the open desert area. I knew that, without the rocks for cover and shade, we probably would have been caught by now.

After we ate, Mama told me that we had about a six hour hike to the city, and that we would start as soon as it got dark. She said, "Try to take another nap, because we will probably be up all night again. You'll need your strength with the long walk ahead."

I tried to fall asleep, but I just couldn't. I began to get extremely restless about an hour after we ate. I felt like I needed to move around. Mama tried to keep me occupied by talking about everything from when I was a baby, to my first day of school.

That afternoon we saw two more patrols off in the distance. We could see the dust that the trucks kicked up on the barren, flat land. I thought to myself that Mama was smart to have us only travel at night.

While we were waiting in the desert that afternoon, I couldn't help feeling like we were fugitives on the run. I felt like we had just robbed a store or something and were trying to get away. It wasn't a pleasant feeling at all. I had never done anything against the law before, and I'm sure Mama hadn't either, before this all started. But we were desperate, and desperate people do desperate things. We waited in the same place the entire day. It was excruciating staying behind those rocks for twelve hours in that stifling heat.

When nightfall finally came, my legs were cramped up like never before. Mama waited until it was fully dark out and said, "It's time to go to our new life." When she spoke those words to me, I felt like they would be embedded in my mind forever. Those words symbolized freedom to me, and the better life that I always dreamed about. I longed for the moment that we would be in our own house in El Paso. I was determined, even though we had a long journey ahead of us. I wasn't about to get discouraged.

I was excited and frightened at the same time when we finally got moving. I could tell my mother was very cautious because we moved in a very unusual pattern. At first we would walk very fast for a short period. Then we would slow down and rest a little, and look around to be sure it was safe. All along, I could see the beautiful city lights off in the distance that seemed to keep my faith alive.

Traveling in the desert at night was frightening, knowing that at any time a border agent could take us into custody. And I didn't even want to think about the snakes and scorpions that live in the desert.

I was also afraid because I knew that someone could see us and rob us, or worse. There was no one around and we wouldn't be able to fight off anyone that wanted to take advantage of two women alone. Mama had money with her, and I knew for sure that people around the border would steal it without a second thought.

About three hours into our journey, I tripped over a small rock in the dark and skinned my knee. Luckily Mama was prepared and had brought a few small pieces of linen for bandages, in case of an emergency. We had to stop for a few minutes so Mama could wipe my knee with the linen and some fresh water from her backpack.

After a few minutes of rest, we were off again as if nothing had happened. Luckily it was just a minor scrape and I wasn't bleeding much. If anything serious would have happened, I am sure we would not have been able to get help. We would have surely perished.

It was one of the risks of taking this journey. We just had to press on and dismiss the risk as an obstacle in the way of our new beginning. We had to stay alert and be aware of our surroundings. We just had to continue on, step by step.

Mama was clear about one thing: we weren't about to take any chances after we had come this far. There was no turning back. We were determined to make it at all costs. I truly felt in my heart that our new life was waiting for us.

As we got closer and closer, I could feel the excitement of our lifelong dream coming true. I could picture all the things I had hoped for my entire life waiting for us in El Paso. It looked as if we were finally going to get the break we had been waiting for.

After about seven hours of walking, we finally approached the highway leading to El Paso. Mama and I hugged each other and jumped around in excitement. She said, "We are going to have to try to hitch a ride the rest of the way into the city."

She had a map that she had gone over many times. The only thing that now stood between us and all our dreams was a ride into the city. She said, "It is a good thing that we both speak some English, because it will help us get a ride."

We waited on the side of the road until just before the sun came up. Without hesitation, Mama went right to edge of the road and stuck her thumb out. She said, "It is dangerous to hitch a ride, but we have no choice. Hitchhiking is an easy way for the border patrol to pick up illegal immigrants, so we will have to be very careful."

After about ten minutes, a semi truck rumbling down the road saw us and pulled over about a hundred yards in front of us. As we ran toward the truck, my heart pounded rapidly. I was starting to feel that frightened, sick, anxious feeling again. When we got close to the truck, I noticed it was fairly new, with a blue cab. On the back was some sort of heavy machinery.

As we approached the cab, the driver rolled down his window and asked us, "Where are you going?"

Before Mama said anything, I noticed that she took a good look at him, probably to see if it was safe. With a heavy accent she answered, "Into the city."

The driver said, "That's where I'm going. Hop in." Mama turned to me and nodded in approval then we hopped into the cab.

I noticed the driver was a heavy-set man with thick eyeglasses. He was very light-skinned and was in desperate need of a shave. He must have been on the road for some time, because his old blue jeans and red t-shirt looked wrin-kled and slept in.

As soon as we got in, he pulled back onto the highway and we were off. He asked, "Where are you going specifical-ly?"

Mama said, "Front Street."

He said, "I'm not going that far, but I can drop you off about six miles away."

Mama said, "That will be great!"

There was a noticeable difference in the way he spoke versus the way we did. He spoke English clearly and con-cisely. We spoke broken English with a heavy accent. Suddenly I worried that he would be suspicious of us and find out we were illegal immigrants. Our speech could be a dead giveaway that we were from Mexico.

Just then the driver asked us, "What are you going to do in the city?"

My mother said, "We are going to see a friend."

All of a sudden I got nervous because he asked us where we lived. My mother said, "Out in the country."

I began to fear for our safety. When I looked at him again, though, he seemed harmless enough. I didn't want anyone to know that we were from Mexico, so I didn't say a word. My mother had told me many times to say as little as possible. She had said, "If someone finds out we are here illegally, we could end up in jail and be sent back to Mexico." I certainly did not want to go back to Uncle Carlos, so I kept quiet.

Just then Mama purposely changed the subject. She asked the driver, "What are you hauling?"

He said, "Machines to make parts for lawn equipment. I don't know that much about it. I just pick them up and deliver them."

The truck ride was only about twenty minutes, but it seemed like it lasted forever.

The anxiety and fear I felt during that ride was comparable to when I first arrived at Santa Maria's. I was shaky and breathing hard off and on the entire way. I don't think Mama even noticed because she was busy keeping an eye on the driver. I knew she didn't trust him and I was sure she wasn't going to let anything happen to us after how far we had already come. We were finally in the United States and she wanted to be sure we were not going to get sent back.

The closer we got to the city, the more amazed I was. I had never seen a big city like El Paso before. I had seen Juarez, but it was nothing like this. I had heard many wonderful stories about Mexico City, but they were only stories. This was the real thing. All I could do was stare out the window in amazement at all the traffic and the buildings. It was truly astonishing to me how large the buildings looked.

The driver finally pulled over and said, "This is as close as I can take you." We thanked him as we hopped out of the large cab.

I couldn't help but wonder if he knew we were illegal immigrants because he seemed a little suspicious. But he wished us good luck as he shut the door.

I felt a great sense of relief as the truck finally pulled away. Mama immediately took out a stack of papers and began to study a map. After a short pause she turned to me and said, "We must go that way. We need to get moving as fast as possible if we're going to meet our contact."

We walked for about an hour, which seemed to go by quickly. I was busy looking around the entire time, taking in the sights and sounds of a large, fast-paced city. It was so different from the country life of rural Mexico, I hardly knew what to think.

Mama finally said, "I'm hungry. It is time to stop and eat." We stopped at a place with a red and white sign called Burger King. I had never been in any type of restaurant like it before.

Mama said, "This is a common place to eat. It isn't expensive, and I think you will really like the food."

We were very hungry from our long journey. I ordered a huge hamburger with cheese and french fries. The food tasted great! I never knew that a restaurant like that even existed. I was a long way from the life I once knew. Everything seemed so strange and new and exciting.

After we finished our meal, Mama didn't waste any time. We began walking again just as we had before. The pain in my feet from two days of continuous walking was excruciating, but Mama told me we had to press on. She said. "We have about four more miles to go. If we are persistent, we can make it in about an hour and a half."

My feet were throbbing worse than ever by the time we got to the meeting place. I figured that we had walked about thirty-eight miles in about two days and I felt it. It seemed like so long ago when we were on those hot, dry, flat plains sneaking over the border. So much had happened in such a short period of time that it didn't seem like it was only yesterday.

I thought about all of the new sights I had seen along the way and I felt a sudden sense of jubilation. I felt encouraged and had a great sense of hope. I knew we had a long task ahead of us still, but I felt relieved.

Just then my train of thought was interrupted by my mother saying, "We are here."

When I looked up, I was surprised to see that we were standing in front of a bar called Lucky's. I asked, "Are you sure we are in the right place?"

She said, "Yes."

It was a small, run-down place with a wooden exterior. It sat between a party store and a car wash, and it looked pathetic. Mama told me to wait outside. She said, "Sit down on the bench in front of the car wash. I have to go inside to meet my contact. If you really need me, you can come in. Don't talk to anyone and try not to look suspicious."

Normally, she wouldn't take a chance on leaving me alone out there, but we had been taking a lot of chances since we had left Mexico. I said, "I'm not about to talk to anyone, so you don't have to worry." I wasn't about to take a chance on someone finding out we were here illegally. We had come too far to go back now. Then she walked into Lucky's and left me sitting there.

I enjoyed watching all the people taking their cars into the car wash. It was the type of car wash where you had to get out of your car as it went through the wash. The people would inspect their cars at the end, before they got in and drove away.

It was very peculiar when people drove by me like I didn't even exist, like I was a statue or something. People were just preoccupied with themselves. It was a fast-paced city where people apparently didn't have time to be bothered with anyone else.

My mother was in Lucky's for what seemed like an eternity. After about twenty minutes, I was becoming increasingly concerned for her safety. It looked like a seedy place and, after all, she was in there to do something illegal. We really had no choice because this was where her contact was. We had both made the decision that we were not going back at any cost.

When she finally emerged, she had a smile on her face. I was relieved. She immediately said, "Let's go. Next we need to find a place to stay." She paused for a moment and said, "I had to give a man in Lucky's $400."

Amazed, I asked, "For what?"

We stopped walking and she said, "All right, Maria, if you must know, Linda loaned me nearly $2,000 and I had $900 saved. The money is for us to get started here in the United States. The man I went to see set us up with a place to live. He told me where I can get a job, and he also arranged for me to get an identification card. The card will have our new address on it and it will be very helpful if anyone questions us. It's called a state identification card and is a type of proof that we belong here. Now we must walk a few more miles to an apartment building where I hope we can get a place to stay. I'll be meeting the manager there."

My feet were throbbing with pain after just a few minutes of walking. I tried to focus on the city to get my mind off the pain. I figured I could only walk a few more blocks before I would collapse.

Everything was so new and fresh to me, I couldn't believe it. Here we were in the United States, going to get our own place to live. I was so excited, I quickly forgot about my aching feet.

After about an hour's walk, we arrived at an apartment complex on the outskirts of town. They were aluminum, two-story apartment buildings in desperate need of refurbishing. I couldn't believe there were so many units — 125 in all.

The buildings from the outside looked old and decrepit. The siding was a discolored yellow with pieces missing here and there. The trim was a dirty white color with the paint peeling off in most areas. The window screens were ripped and torn, and a few of the windows were broken. The parking lot was old and cracked with potholes in many spots.

Even through the place looked run-down, it still was a welcome sight. By the time we arrived, my feet felt like they were going to fall off. I just wanted to stop and rest. My mother found the manager's office and walked right in like she owned the place. I thought to myself, *I wish I had her strength and confidence.* She was a trooper, a real fireball, and I knew it.

My stomach had that uneasy feeling again, but I reluctantly followed Mama right into the office. When she approached the desk, without hesitation she said, "I need to see Pedro Rodriguez."

The woman politely said, "He will be back in a minute or two." She told us to have a seat, so we sat down directly across from her in a couple of old wooden chairs.

She was a rather heavy woman who looked like she was part Mexican and part something else. She looked different from the people I was used to seeing in Mexico. Her eyes were dark brown and she had chubby cheeks. She had on a purple shirt with white sweatpants.

As we were waiting for Pedro to return, she began to ask us some questions. She asked us if we were from El Paso or if we were from Mexico. My mother and I didn't say a word. Then she asked us if we were going to rent an apartment. Mama said, "If it's all right, we prefer to wait for Pedro."

The woman said, "You know, it's all right if you tell me. I won't say anything."

Just then, Pedro walked in. I breathed a sigh of relief when I saw him. He was a rather short man, about five feet, six inches tall, and somewhat overweight, with light brown hair and brown eyes.

I was glad he was there because all the questions the secretary was asking us made me uncomfortable. Mama proceeded to tell him who we were and who sent us, when he abruptly cut her off. He rudely said, "A one bedroom will be $450 a month and a two bedroom will be $575 a month. I'll need $450 for the first month's rent, $450 for a security deposit, and $200 for a non-refundable application fee."

My mother just looked at him for a moment. Then he added, "I need it in cash. If you are more than seven days late with the rent, you owe me $75 more. If you are seven days late with the rent, you'll get an eviction notice. By the way, I always win when there is an eviction."

Mama said, "I need a minute." Then she went into the bathroom for what seemed like an eternity. When she came out, she had a handful of money. She said, "Here it is, all of it."

Pedro sat down and started counting. When he was done, he said in a pleased voice, "Yes, it is all here, the entire $1,100." He handed it back to my mother for some reason.

I just sat there with an uneasy feeling in my stomach. I had never seen that much money in my life and I was nervous.

Mama asked, "Can we see the unit?"

Pedro said, "Sure." Just then I noticed that he was missing two of his front teeth, and that he had a tattoo of a shark on his arm. He was a bit scary-looking after I got a real good look at him.

He told the secretary to get the key so he could show us unit C-12. It was just around the corner from the office. Surprisingly, the apartment was fairly clean. It had white walls with dirt stains near the floor. The floors had brown tile throughout the entire unit. Mama asked if they would put carpeting in for her.

Pedro said, "We never put carpeting in for anyone. People always end up ruining it and that costs too much money anyway. Every unit has the same tile, throughout the entire building. What you see is what you get. There will be no changes."

My mother didn't make a sound. She knew we needed a place to stay and wasn't about to complain.

The bathroom was so small you could hardly move around in it. It had a shower, a sink, a toilet, and a mirror. That was it. You couldn't even take two steps without being out of the bathroom and into the hall. The kitchen had a built-in stove, with no refrigerator or dishwasher. The living room was extremely small, with an old, gray couch that was probably left by the old tenants.

In the back of the unit was a small bedroom that was a bit dark and dingy. It had possibilities, though, with some cleaning and minor repairs. I thought to myself that it really wasn't that bad. With a little painting and cleaning it could be nice.

When we got back to the office, Mama told Pedro that she thought $450 was a little high for that unit. He looked at her with a very peculiar look on his face and said, "You really aren't in a position to bargain, now are you? I know you need this place really bad and have no other options. But since you have guts and you seem like you won't be any trouble for me, I'll give you the unit for $440 and that's final. Take it or leave it."

My mother sighed and said, "We will take it." She handed him $1,080 after taking out $20 because of the lower rent she bargained for. He said, "I have some papers for you to sign back at the office. It will take about ten minutes."

When we were done, he handed my mother the key and said, "Remember, if you don't pay the rent, you'll be gone so fast it will make your head spin. Save your excuses for someone who cares. Do you understand?"

Mama said, "Yes," then she turned away and walked out of the office. I hurried after her.

As we walked to the unit, Mama was clearly excited, rambling on about all the work we were going to do on the apartment. As soon as we got inside, she gave me the biggest hug imaginable. Then she said, "We made it! We actually made it!"

The hug she gave me felt incredible. I felt like I would remember that moment for the rest of my life. A huge weight had been taken off my shoulders and I felt a great sense of relief. I actually started to cry.

Mama asked me what was wrong. I said, "I'm just so happy I felt like crying."

She said, "I'm happy too, Maria. I'm so proud of you for being so brave during the entire crossing. I love you so much."

I felt so thankful for everything Mama had done for me. I was so grateful that I was going to help her any way I could.

The apartment wasn't the mansion I had dreamed about all my life, but I wasn't about to complain. I couldn't help thinking that things were finally looking up for us. I just wanted to be careful, because every other time I had thought things were looking up, things had seemed to deteriorate.

Mama said, "You know Maria, we have a lot of work to do. I have to get a job right away and we have to get you enrolled in school. Also, this apartment needs a lot of work to make it clean and livable."

She smiled at me and added, "But don't worry. We will have this place in great shape in no time at all."

Then she sat down and said, "Let's see how much money we have left. We started out with $2,900. I gave $400 to the driver to take us to the border. I gave $400 to the man at Lucky's. I gave $1,080 to Pedro for the apartment. That leaves us with $1,020. That's not bad." She paused for a moment and said, "That was all the money Linda and I had saved. I will have to pay her back as soon as I can. It's awful that your Aunt Linda puts up with everything that she does. Carlos is such a jerk and doesn't deserve her. We need to pray for her every night."

I said I would, and told her I was tired. She said, "Let's get some sleep and we will go from there." We took a four hour nap that day. That nasty old couch felt so comforting to me that afternoon. After the border crossing and the walk through the city, I was exhausted.

When we woke up, we both took a long shower. I never felt so invigorated as I did after getting two days' worth of dirt and grime off my body. Then Mama and I walked to a store that was a couple blocks away. We bought non-perishable food items and some cleaning supplies.

We spent the entire evening talking and cleaning. I felt proud that night. I felt as if maybe, just maybe, God had heard my plea for help. I felt that maybe things were going to be decent for us, for the first time since my father had died.

Everything was so different from what I pictured the United States to be. I knew we would have to work hard, but somehow I felt it would eventually work out. We just had to be very careful not to let anyone know we were here illegally. The last thing we wanted was to get deported. That night I prayed with great intensity and thanked God for bringing us this far.

— 13 —

The next morning Mama was up early. She said, "I have to go see a man about getting our identification cards. I'll have to pay him another $200, and that will leave us with just $800. It is crucial to get those identification cards as soon as possible.

"I'll be gone several hours. Do not go out. There is food in the kitchen. If you get bored, you can clean some more." Then she hurried off. I spent the entire morning and part of the afternoon, alone in the apartment, cleaning. Mama got home just before 3:00 p.m.

When she walked in she said, "I have great news! I got a job. I got a real job and it should be steady, too."

An incredible feeling of relief came over me. I was so happy that I ran to my mother and jumped on her. She was so surprised that we both fell on the floor.

She smiled at me and said, "I'll be working at a restaurant called the Cross City Diner. It's a small family restaurant about three miles away. I'll be a waitress there. The starting pay is $4.50 an hour plus tips. The owner agreed to pay me in cash, so I get to keep it all. They call it 'under the table.' It means I don't need a green card or anything."

We were so excited that we forgot that Mama had three bags with clothing and some food that she had set down when she first walked in the door. After a moment or two, when we calmed down, she said, "I have more good news. We should be getting our state identification cards tomorrow. I had to give the man pictures of us today."

I was so excited that I forgot to mention that I had cleaned all day. My mother noticed, though, and said, "Nice job on the apartment, Maria."

I just said "thank you" and smiled. I felt like things were truly falling into place for us. I thought all those long nights praying just might be paying off.

Even so, I felt a little dishonest, knowing that my mother was getting fake identification for us. I felt like it was wrong to work illegally, even though it was necessary. A few minutes later, I mentioned how I felt.

She said, "I know I have always taught you to be honest. I know that doing the honest thing is always the best. But I feel this is an exception to the rule. This is something that we really have to do. I love you, Maria, and I love God, too. I really feel like this is our calling and that we must do this. You do understand, don't you?"

I just nodded and said, "Yes."

Then she said, "Tomorrow I'll start at the diner at 10:00 a.m. Before work I'm going to register you for school. The state identifications will help. I have a copy of our lease, which will also help. So tomorrow, I'll be gone most of the day. You'll have to keep yourself busy. I don't want you going out at all until I get home. I bought an inexpensive radio, and you can clean tomorrow again."

That night was one of the first nights I'd felt good before bed since Mama had been arrested. I felt like maybe, just maybe, our dreams were going to come true. I still prayed, thanking God that night just as I normally did. I thanked him for helping us get over the border that lonesome night in the desert, and for keeping us safe throughout our journey. I thanked him for bringing my mother back to me and for helping her find a job. I thanked him for all that he had done in the past for us. I also asked him to continue to help us in the future.

All in all, it had been a fabulous day. Especially for my mother, who seemed more determined and focused than ever, now that she had a job. Before she was worried about paying the rent. Now she would have enough money to pay the rent and buy the things that we needed. The last thing I thought that night, before falling asleep, was how lucky I was to be living in the United States.

I slept soundly that night on the old couch. I woke to the sound of Mama moving about. I still felt tired from all the sleepless, worrisome nights I'd had in the past, especially, that long and terrifying night we'd spent in the desert near the border.

When I finally got up, Mama said, "I'm going to Lucky's to get our identification cards. After that I'm going to register you for school."

Before she left she said, "The man at Lucky's is going to provide us with a fake lease that showed that we had been living in San Diego, California, before El Paso." She told me she had to pay $200 more when the man delivered the identification cards and the lease.

My mother had it all figured out. She had a job. We had a place to live. We were going to have a prior address so that if anyone did question us, we would have all the right answers. She explained that it was crucial that we stuck with our story and made it convincing, because if we didn't, we could easily get deported. Our story was that we had moved from San Diego because we wanted to find a less expensive place to live.

She said, "I don't want to lie because it is wrong, but we have no other choice. We have to maintain some stability to be able to stay in the United States."

That day went by slowly. Things got real boring after my chores were done. Thank goodness Mama bought that radio. That was the only thing that kept me from going stir-crazy that day.

I listened to a station that played American and Mexican music, and I really enjoyed it. A few times I actually danced. Antonio had taught me to dance a little back home, but he only taught me a few steps and I always improvised from there.

I missed Antonio so much. He had been such a good friend and was always so nice to us. I wondered if I would ever see him again. I kept telling myself I would, but I wasn't so sure.

I just fooled around the rest of the day. It felt good not having to worry so much. It was actually fun just relaxing and listening to the music. I had not had any real fun, without worrisome concerns, since I was back home playing soccer with my friends.

When Mama came home, she was very excited. She showed me our state identification cards and said, "The pictures were old ones but they'll do fine." They looked authentic to me.

She said, "I really enjoyed my first day on the job. Things are going to work out for me there. The work is great and I really like my boss. I made $48 in tips in just seven hours."

Then she told me about school. She told me that it was a big school with a gym, a huge lunchroom, and a computer room. I had never seen a real computer before, but I knew what they were. She said, "The school seemed strict and the children seemed well-behaved. You'll be taught English and Spanish. The principal appeared to be nice and genuinely caring. And guess what, Maria, they have a real soccer team."

My mouth just fell open. *A soccer team*, I thought, *wow!* Mama smiled and said, "You start Wednesday. I gave them the former address in San Diego that the man at Lucky's gave me. Everything should check out. I must remind you to be careful what you say. You must tell people we lived at 1644 Lexington Avenue, apartment number 14, in San Diego, California. You know if people find out we are here illegally, we could get deported. I would never want you to lie about anything, but this is important. Do you understand?"

I took a deep breath and said, "Yes." So our stage was set. As far as anyone was concerned, we were from San Diego, California. I didn't want to lie about anything because I was a terrible liar. I knew I had to, though. I felt horrible the rest of the night, knowing that I would have to lie.

Wednesday came quickly and I was ready to start school. Mama worked all week and she seemed settled at the diner. We actually had steady money coming in for the first time since I could remember. Mama bought me a new pair of jeans and a new shirt to wear on my first day. I don't remember ever having a new outfit in my entire life.

As I approached the school that morning, I'll never forget the feeling of pure astonishment that filled my body. When I saw the enormous size of the building, I was invigorated. It was a big brick building with a green metal roof that looked almost like a mansion. It made the school back in Juarez look like a dollhouse. The front door was dark-tinted glass with a shiny silver handle. The gymnasium ceiling was about twelve feet higher than the rest of the building. To the sides of the massive building were soccer fields, football fields, and a baseball diamond.

I'd never seen anything like it before. I just couldn't believe it. My mother had told me it was amazing, but I had no idea it would be like this. I had a brief feeling of excitement and anxiety as Mama walked me to the doors that day. She had arranged a meeting with the principal that morning before school.

The principal's name was Mr. Newman. He was a short bald man, with a blue suit coat and a grey shirt on that was filled out by his potbelly stomach. He had a nice smile and a calm look about him.

When we went into his office, I noticed there was another person in there waiting — an immigration officer, dressed in a uniform. He had a badge and a gun and he didn't look friendly.

After Mr. Newman introduced us, the agent asked me where we were from. Mama started to answer, but the agent said, "Sorry, Miss Perez. I asked Maria."

Again he asked, "Where are you from?" My body froze. My legs felt like blocks of ice. I managed to timidly say that we were from San Diego, California.

The agent said, "Where in San Diego are you from?"

I blurted out the address: "1644 Lexington Avenue, apartment number 14."

Then he looked at a few papers and said, "I'm sorry for any convenience. We are just doing our job. You can never be too careful. I interview most of the new students that come here, just to make sure everything is on the up-and-up." He paused for a moment and said, "Welcome to the school, Maria. I hope you like it here. You will fit in well with all of the other students."

Just then Mr. Newman's secretary, Mrs. Sinclair, came to the door and said, "Mr. Pablo is here to see you now, sir." I was so relieved that the principal had another meeting. That immigration officer frightened me beyond belief. I was just glad he believed us. All the hard work of coming over the border, and the sacrifices we made, could have all been for nothing. If I had just said the wrong thing, we could have been on our way back to Mexico. Mama and I had rehearsed where we were supposedly from many times in the days before my first day of school.

I had never flat-out lied to a grown-up before. I felt saddened and guilty as Mrs. Sinclair walked me to my first class. For now, I knew I just had to live with that lie. I was afraid it would turn into more lies eventually.

Now I had something new to worry about. I worried that the immigration agent would do some checking and find out we were not from San Diego. I worried about my mother, who was still in the office with the agent. So far my first day of school was off to a nerve-wracking start.

As I approached my first classroom, Mrs. Sinclair handed me a schedule, a locker number, a combination, and a map of the school. She said, "This is your first class, pre-algebra."

I didn't want to ask any questions because I was still so nervous from the immigration officer's questions. I'd never had a locker before, or separate classrooms. At home we always had the same teacher for all our subjects. Wow! Were things ever different in the United States.

Right before I entered my first class, I felt lost and out of place. I was very concerned that I wouldn't fit in.

I wondered if I could pull off this terrible lie that I was living, or if I would be caught, humiliated, and sent back to Mexico. I was determined to do what I had to so I could stay here. I was somewhat proficient with the English language, but not to the level that American children were. I just would have to work extra hard to get to their level.

When I walked in the room, I couldn't believe it. The classroom was huge, probably three times as large as my classroom back home. It was very bright and friendly looking, and had a lot of windows letting in the sunlight. It was cleanly painted white and had a huge chalkboard that spanned the entire front of the classroom. The floors were tiled and shiny like glass. I was awestruck. This was a far cry from what I was used to.

I was a few minutes early, so Mrs. Sinclair introduced me to the teacher of my homeroom. Her name was Mrs. Harris. She was tall and thin, and she had blonde hair with blue eyes. She did not look like a teacher to me at all. I thought she looked more like a model than anything else.

Mrs. Sinclair said, "If you need anything, Maria, or if you have any trouble at all, come and see me. I'll be more than happy to help you."

The other kids started coming in and taking their seats. After Mrs. Harris introduced me, she quickly assigned me a seat and told me to follow along as best as I could. She said, "I'll help you after class or after school if you need it."

She started class and handed out our first assignment. I was lost that morning. The math she gave us was way ahead of what I was doing back home. I knew school was going to be a challenge, but I hadn't expected it to be this difficult. I had always been a good student and I was sure I would conquer this math in time.

The other classes I had were English, social studies, science, and physical education. It was such a shock going from class to class that I felt a little anxiety-stricken again. I wasn't to the point of an anxiety attack, but I was definitely overwhelmed.

My final class of the day was Physical Education. When I walked into the gymnasium I couldn't believe my eyes. It was like a huge building all by itself. It had a basketball court with a full waxed tile floor. It had bleachers and space on the basketball court to play volleyball, floor hockey, or any other sport. It totally astonished me.

That day we played basketball for the entire hour. I had never played before, so I was a little shaky, trying to remember the rules. I had so much fun that afternoon in the gymnasium that I didn't want to leave.

My first day of school was overwhelming, but ended up being rather fun. I knew I was going to struggle with the level of schoolwork here. I would just have to adapt as well as I could. I felt like I had found my place and I was somewhat satisfied. I still felt enormous stress, knowing I was the new girl there. I was so far behind all the other students that I felt like I would never catch up. But I was happy at school for the first time in quite a while.

The discouraging thought of the immigration officer at our school didn't sit well with me, though. I wondered if I'd have to talk with him again. I would just have to wait it out and keep praying every night for help. I felt like I had found my home and there was no way I was going back. I was determined to stay in the United States and I would work as hard as I could to ensure our secret would not be discovered.

After school, Mama told me she had a good day at work. She asked me how school was. I told her, "I'll have to work very hard and stay after school to get help every day to catch up with the other students."

The smile she gave me at that moment was incredible. I will never forget it. It was as if she was given a gift like no other. She looked so enthusiastic and gave me a huge hug. Then she said, "Things appear to be turning around for us. I'm so proud of you because you are so determined and focused. You remind me of your father. I love you."

Just then a tear rolled down my cheek. It was a different kind of tear than what I had cried so many times since her arrest. Those few weeks had been the most fearful time of my life. I was happy now, but I knew if Immigration got hold of us, it could be all over in a moment. I realized we would have to live in fear for the rest of our lives. If we got caught, we would be worse off than ever.

I spent the next two weeks working with my teachers after school to get caught up. I spent every evening doing homework. My life was exclusively focused on school.

The only reprieve I had was when my new friends Anna and Isabel ate lunch with me every day. We were in two classes together and we were becoming good friends. I actually looked forward to school, even though it was very difficult at first. It helped that I had a couple of friends who were willing to help me with my homework, or with studying when I needed it.

Most things at school were definitely better here than in Mexico. The facilities were incredible. The teachers were extremely helpful and appeared to have a genuine concern for the well-being of each student. It was such a positive atmosphere. I was still a little intimidated by the computer lab, though. I'd never worked on a computer before I came here and it was going to take some time to get used to it. physical education class was my favorite. I loved sports and couldn't wait to play something different each week.

It appeared to me that when you are living with a constant struggle to survive, like we were in Mexico, you become more motivated to achieve when you are given the opportunity for success. This is why I was working so hard to catch up with the other students.

One of the things that surprised me the most about my new school was that there were so many kids from so many different cultures. Most of the children were Mexican, but some were white, some were black, and some were even from Japan or India.

After six weeks I was finally getting caught up with the other students. I worked every day after school to accomplish this. It was a very difficult task, but well worth it.

Eight weeks after we crossed the border, it appeared all my prayers had been answered. We had an apartment in El Paso. I was doing well in school. My mother was working steadily at the restaurant and I had made two close friends. The teachers were friendly and appeared to take a liking to me because of my determination. But every once in a while, a memory of Mexico would flash back into my mind. Then I would remember we were still illegal immigrants and at any time we could be forced to go back.

One day, something awful happened that really made Mama and I worry. I'd had a good day at school and was walking home with my friend Anna. When Anna said goodbye, I strolled up to our apartment, took out my key, and noticed the door was open. I peered in and saw that everything was messy and out of place. My heart raced as I walked into the bedroom and saw my mother's things scattered about.

Right then I started breathing hard. Anxiety took over my body as my heart raced. I was having another panic attack. Thoughts of whether my mother was safe entered my mind. Had she been deported? Was she hurt? Had she been beaten? I hyperventilated right then and there. I kneeled to the floor and tried breathing steadily. I knew I had to bring my breathing under control, so I spent the next couple minutes calming myself down.

After I regained my composure, I thought the best thing I could do was to run over to Mama's work and see if she was all right. I ran out the door and over to the diner, worrying the entire way. I wondered if I would ever see her again. When I arrived at the restaurant and bolted through the door, I was panicking again. Was she all right?

As I gasped for air, I saw Mama serving some customers their meals as if nothing was wrong. I ran up to her in utter disarray and began crying. She asked, "What's wrong?" as I firmly clung to her. Panting heavily, I managed to blurt out, "I thought you were gone!"

She said, "Gone, Maria? Where would I go?"

As my breathing began to level out, I told her how I went home after school and found the apartment a mess. I told her I thought she'd been hurt or something.

A very surprised look darted across Mama's face. She told me to wait a minute as she turned to her boss and asked, "Can I leave a half hour early? I think our apartment was broken into."

He said, "By all means. Go and take care of it."

Broken into, I thought, *oh no*. It never occurred to me that someone had broken in. As we hurried back to our apartment, Mama kept on saying, "I hope they didn't take the rent money."

When we got home, she immediately ran into her bedroom, went over to the ransacked dresser, and said, "No!" Then she pulled the dresser out from the wall. There behind it, taped under the backside, was an envelope still attached where she'd left it. She took a deep breath and said, "Thank you, God." She told me because we had been buying all the necessities we needed over the last eight weeks, we didn't have much left over. If that rent money had been gone, we would have been in big trouble.

Even though the thieves took a few items, like the radio, and the apartment was in utter chaos, we still felt like it could have been much worse. Mama said, "I didn't open a bank account because you need a social security number to do so. If I tried, they might find out we are here illegally and we could have been deported. So I had to keep our money here in a safe place. We can't call the police because we can't draw any attention to ourselves. We will just have to put a better lock on the door."

I felt discouraged and totally violated. The fact that we couldn't go the police didn't sit well with me at all. Mama said, "Don't worry, because thieves never come back to the same place. It is too easy for them to get caught."

I asked her, "Are we were safe here in El Paso?"

She said, "Yes, of course."

I felt a little better knowing this was an isolated incident and that the thieves would not be back. We spent most of that evening cleaning up the place. We both talked that night about how thankful we were to be where we were. Mama didn't seem to mind much about the break-in because they didn't get our rent money.

That night I prayed with the same intensity I had at Santa Maria's. I thanked God that my mother was all right and that we were safe. I also asked for his help to ensure that we would remain safe and not get deported.

I'd felt like we were finally getting ahead, until that break-in happened. The next few weeks were spent recovering and accumulating things we needed that we lost during that unfortunate incident. I wondered if we would ever recover from the setback. I worried that we might get robbed again.

My mother was working six days a week, making enough to pay the rent and buy the things we needed. There wasn't much money left over at the end of the month, but we always had food. It was always in the back of our minds that at any time we could be deported and sent back to Mexico. Everything we were working so hard for could be gone in a moment. Living in constant fear was discouraging. We always had to be careful what we said and what we did. It was a fear that every illegal immigrant lives with every day.

— 14 —

Fourteen weeks had gone by since the day we crossed the border. All our struggles and triumphs came to a climax on Christmas morning when Mama said, "I have a big surprise for you."

I was surprised just to see the wrapped packages. The first two presents I opened were clothes, which I desperately needed. She bought me two brand-new outfits, which made me very happy. I had never received so many pieces of clothing in one day before in my life.

Then Mama brought a box in from the other room. It was wrapped in red wrapping paper with paw prints all over it. She had a great big smile on her face. My heart raced with excitement as I looked the box over.

She asked, "Well, are you going to open it?"

I said, "Yes, I am." I just wanted to wait a little and enjoy the moment. As I ripped the paper off and opened the box, I couldn't believe it. It was a nineteen-inch TV. In all my wildest dreams, I never thought it was possible. As a tear rolled down my cheek I said, "How did you get it? Mama, you shouldn't have. The rent is more important."

Then she said something I never imagined possible. She said, "Maria, the rent is paid up. I have worked hard for the last few months and we deserve this. I also have something else to tell you. I've met someone I really like a lot, a man."

My jaw dropped and I repeated, "A man?"

She said, "Yes. His name is Cristofer. I met him soon after I started working at the restaurant. He is a decent man with a good job. He is a car mechanic and is very responsible. He has treated me very well thus far. I have never told you about him because I wasn't sure about him. Well, I'm pretty sure now.

"I know what you are thinking, Maria. I just want you to know that no one, I mean no one will ever take the place of your father. He meant the world to me and he will always hold a special place in my heart. But he has been gone for over ten years now. I like Cristofer, and I would really be happy if you gave him a chance."

I was stunned and I didn't know what to say. I gave her a huge hug and said, "If you really like him, I'll give him a chance."

Mama said, "Good, because he is coming over to meet you today."

My eyes got as huge as balloons that were over-filled with air. "Today?" I asked.

She said, "Yes. He will be here at 1:00."

I felt excited and a little nervous. Mama and I spent a whole hour picking up the apartment and getting ready for Cristofer to come over. When it was time, our little place was just perfect.

Mama seemed nervous and a little impatient as we waited for him to arrive. She had a ham for dinner cooking in our small oven.

Finally, after what seemed like an eternity, there was a gentle knock at the door. As my mother went to answer it, I felt like there were butterflies flying around in my stomach.

When Cristofer walked in, he smiled at my mother and she smiled back. This made me feel a little uncomfortable at first. He immediately came over to me and said, "You must be Maria." He smiled as he reached out his hand to shake mine.

I smiled back and said, "I'm pleased to meet you." He was about six feet tall, with a thin build and dark hair. He was clean-shaven and had a very nice warm smile.

The nervousness I felt before melted away. For some reason I felt comfortable around him. He said, "Here, Maria. This is for you." He gave me a present wrapped in green paper with a pink ribbon around it.

I looked at Mama and she nodded with approval. When I opened it, I was very excited. It was a book: *Treasure Island* by Robert Louis Stevenson. He said, "Your mother told me that you love to read, so I bought you a great classic."

I said, "Thank you," and looked away because I didn't know what else to say.

He sat down and we spent the rest of that Christmas talking, eating, and having a great time. The meal that day was one of the best I ever remembered. That night I thanked God for everything I had and fell asleep easily.

Mama ended up falling in love with Cristofer. A year later they were married. Cristofer and I became great friends. I truly liked him. My mother was right, he was a good man. He helped me get on my school's soccer team, and even helped me practice every day. It was like he was an angel sent to help us.

We ended up moving into his house in El Paso. Even though it wasn't the mansion I had dreamed about back in Mexico, it sure beat where we were living when we first came to the United States. It was a three bedroom ranch, with two bathrooms and a large, two car attached garage.

In my eyes, I guess it was a mansion. I realized that it wasn't the size of the house that mattered. It was how peaceful and happy our household was that counted. I felt safe and confident for the first time in my life.

Cristofer and Mama seemed so happy. It felt great knowing that she had found someone that she truly cared about. Mama and I still talked about my father often, though. We promised each other we would never forget the great man that he was.

Cristofer could never replace my father, but I liked him and he made Mama happy. He was so caring when he helped me with my schoolwork, and he was so kind to me, he treated me like I was his own child. He even ended up buying us a ping-pong table.

The thing I liked the best about him, though, was that he was always willing to help my mother or me, no matter how busy he was. He truly loved Mama and, for the first time in my life, I felt safe and content with things the way they were. It seemed like my whole life had been spent living in fear. Now I felt relieved. I didn't have to worry about being deported or being evicted ever again.

Since Cristofer was a United States citizen, and my mother was married to him, we were able to apply for United States citizenship. Mama said it was going to take some time, but we were willing to wait. She was willing to do whatever she had to do, so we would never again have to live in fear of being deported.

I couldn't believe how drastically everything had changed since I was stuck at Santa Maria's Home for Girls. I went from being a confused, homeless girl with no father and a mother who was in jail, to a girl who was doing great in school, who was going to be a United States citizen, who had a stable home with a wonderful stepfather.

I really couldn't ask for anything more. We were very happy. I loved my new life, and I just loved being on my school's soccer team.

I guess all that intense, profuse praying did pay off. God definitely showed us how great he could be. He blessed us with so much, after everything had seemed so hopeless. I guess dreams do come true, they just sometimes take a different path than you expect. I promised myself that I would never forget where I came from. And I would never let a day go by when I would forget to thank God for everything that I had.